"What dat?"

T0221576

Megan pointed to the box.

"It's our Christmas tree," Brooke told the twins.

"Ooh, twee!" Alice clapped her hands.

"Mr. Dean is going to help us put it up, and then we'll decorate it later."

They turned to each other with their mouths in big O's.

"I think they like that idea." Dean grinned.

"I think you're right."

Dean assembled the sections in record time. When he plugged it in, all the lights worked.

"Ooh!" The girls gawked at it.

"I can fluff the branches later." Brooke dragged the empty box out of the way.

"We can get it done now," Dean said. "I don't mind helping."

She turned away at the sudden emotion his words brought up. His kindness kept poking at dormant things inside her. Things she believed she'd lost forever.

The desire to have a partner, to rely on him for help—she wasn't certain she wanted those feelings back, because they only reminded her what she couldn't have. A husband, more children. Not with her health problems.

Jill Kemerer writes novels with love, humor and faith. Besides spoiling her mini dachshund and keeping up with her busy kids, Jill reads stacks of books, lives for her morning coffee and gushes over fluffy animals. She resides in Ohio with her husband and two children. Jill loves connecting with readers, so please visit her website, jillkemerer.com, or contact her at PO Box 2802, Whitehouse, OH 43571.

Books by Jill Kemerer

Love Inspired

Wyoming Legacies

The Cowboy's Christmas Compromise
United by the Twins
Training the K-9 Companion
The Cowboy's Christmas Treasures

Wyoming Ranchers

The Prodigal's Holiday Hope
A Cowboy to Rely On
Guarding His Secret
The Mistletoe Favor
Depending on the Cowboy
The Cowboy's Little Secret

Visit the Author Profile page at LoveInspired.com for more titles.

The Cowboy's Christmas Treasures

JILL KEMERER

LOVE INSPIRED
INSPIRATIONAL ROMANCE

If you purchased this book without a cover you should be aware that this book is stolen property. It was reported as "unsold and destroyed" to the publisher, and neither the author nor the publisher has received any payment for this "stripped book."

LOVE INSPIRED®

INSPIRATIONAL ROMANCE

Recycling programs for this product may not exist in your area.

ISBN-13: 978-1-335-93691-2

The Cowboy's Christmas Treasures

Copyright © 2024 by Ripple Effect Press, LLC

All rights reserved. No part of this book may be used or reproduced in any manner whatsoever without written permission.

Without limiting the author's and publisher's exclusive rights, any unauthorized use of this publication to train generative artificial intelligence (AI) technologies is expressly prohibited.

This is a work of fiction. Names, characters, places and incidents are either the product of the author's imagination or are used fictitiously. Any resemblance to actual persons, living or dead, businesses, companies, events or locales is entirely coincidental.

For questions and comments about the quality of this book, please contact us at CustomerService@Harlequin.com.

® is a trademark of Harlequin Enterprises ULC.

Love Inspired
22 Adelaide St. West, 41st Floor
Toronto, Ontario M5H 4E3, Canada
www.LoveInspired.com

Printed in Lithuania

MIX
Paper | Supporting responsible forestry
FSC® C021394

I can do all things through Christ
which strengtheneth me.
—*Philippians* 4:13

To my incredible husband, Scott.
You never complain about the stacks of books
I leave around the house. You put up with my
irrational fear of spiders. You accept the fact I
need a minimum of five bottles of half-and-half in
the fridge at any given moment, and I never worry
about my car because you're on top of it. I love you.
Merry Christmas!

Chapter One

"He's going to make a good daddy." Brooke Dewitt un-packed empty jars next to her sister-in-law, Reagan Young, who was stirring wax in a warmer at the dining room table. Reagan had offered to help her make homemade candles for Christmas gifts, so Brooke had brought her almost-two-year-old identical twin daughters over to her brother's ranch. The twenty-minute drive from her house in downtown Jewel River, Wyoming, had been easy for mid-November, with no snow yet. Her brother, Marc, was currently in the living room giving Megan and Alice horsey rides. Their squeals and laughter melted her heart into a puddle.

She would do anything for her girls.

"I agree." Reagan rubbed her tiny baby bump. "Marc's going to be a great father."

"He's protective." Brooke hooked a finger around her low ponytail to bring it over her shoulder. "But fun, too."

"You're right about that." Reagan's light brown eyes twin-kled. "He still worries about you, you know."

"I know. I don't mind." She spoke the truth. Marc had been more of a father figure to her than their own dad had been before he'd left when she was twelve and Marc was sixteen. Brooke appreciated the sacrifices Marc and their mother had made over the years, especially the recent ones.

It was hard to believe it had been over eighteen months since Brooke had had the stroke. Being separated from her infant twins for four weeks had devastated her. Almost as much as when she'd found out her husband had died in a helicopter accident while on a training mission overseas. Ross had known she was pregnant, but he hadn't known she was carrying twins.

He'd never met his beautiful girls.

The twins would never have a daddy. She couldn't in good conscience dip her toes in the dating pool, not when she had no plans to get remarried. She wouldn't be having more children, either. The risk of a postpartum stroke was too high. They'd already lost their father. They couldn't lose their mommy, too.

"I still can't believe Ed had a heart attack." Reagan checked the temperature of the wax. Yesterday, local builder Ed McCaffrey had collapsed at his office in town. Brenda, his administrative assistant, had called 911 and performed CPR until the ambulance arrived. She'd likely saved his life.

"I feel so bad for him. It's horrible." A metallic taste developed in her mouth. She hoped he made a full recovery, and not just because he was remodeling her house. "I can't believe it, either."

"I mean, he's always been so full of life. And he's nice. He did an amazing job renovating my chocolate shop. And your mom's bakery."

"He's the best." Brooke couldn't trust herself to speak beyond that. She'd hired Ed's company, McCaffrey Construction, to renovate the three-bedroom home she'd bought this summer in downtown Jewel River. Ed hadn't flinched when she'd explained that she needed the house to be wheelchair accessible in case she had another stroke and ended up with a temporary or permanent disability. By now, most of the renovations had been completed. The halls and doorways had been widened, and vinyl plank flooring had been installed throughout.

But the gutted main bathroom needed tons of work, and the outdoor ramp leading to the back door hadn't been started. If she did have another stroke, she wanted to recover at home. She needed to be prepared for the worst-case scenario.

"When do you think Ed will be released from the hospital?"

Brooke shrugged. "Mom's been texting me with any updates she hears at the bakery, but no one seems to know much at this point."

"Do you think this will set back your renovations?"

"I don't know. Probably." She leaned forward to insert the wicks into the empty jars. "Hopefully, he has a backup plan for emergencies."

"I'm sure he does. And if it takes a few more weeks to finish your house, it takes a few more weeks. Everything will get done eventually." Reagan always knew the right thing to say. Her sister-in-law had a way of easing her mind without even trying.

But what if Ed didn't have a backup plan? Worse, what if he died?

Death was all too real in her world. She'd lost her husband over two years ago and had come close to losing her own life not long after the twins were born. She couldn't bear the thought of kind, capable Ed McCaffrey dying. Thanksgiving was only a week away. And then Christmas. What would it do to his son, Dean?

"The wax is the right temperature. Are you ready to add the fragrance?" Reagan selected a bottle marked Cinnamon and measured it into a small cup on a scale.

"Sure." Brooke rounded the table to stand next to her. "What do I do?"

"Pour this into the wax."

Brooke followed her directions, but it was difficult to concentrate with Ed's health on her mind. Reagan had her repeat the process with the vanilla fragrance.

"How do you feel about Dean staying with you guys?" Brooke asked as Reagan stirred.

"I'm glad." She checked the wax's temperature again. "No one should be alone during those first days following a crisis."

"True. Did he say how long he's staying?" While Dean McCaffrey and Marc had been best friends since elementary school, Brooke had never been close to him. She'd always liked Dean in a little sister type of way. Now that they were both grown-up, she'd noticed him in a mature woman type of way. And it unsettled her.

Dean had been a groomsman in Marc and Reagan's wedding this past spring, but Brooke's hands had been full as a bridesmaid and with the twins being flower girls. She hadn't spent much time with him. He'd been living in Texas for over a decade. He was more handsome now than she remembered. Quieter, too. More reserved. More intriguing.

"Marc seems to think he'll be here for a while," Reagan said. "Maybe Dean will take over your remodeling projects while Ed recovers."

"I can't imagine why he would. Although he does have the experience. He worked for his father all through high school."

"That's what Marc said. Don't worry, it will all work out." She called over her shoulder, "Hey, Marc, when do you think Dean will get here?"

A thumping sound, giggles and footsteps greeted them.

"Soon, I imagine." Marc carried Megan under one arm

and Alice under the other. Their faces were red as they laughed and kicked.

"Unc Mawc, down!" Alice shouted.

"If I set you down, the tickle monster might get you." He grinned at Alice, then at Megan, who squealed.

He carefully set them on the floor, then bent and wiggled his fingers at them. They both took off running, screaming the whole way. Then he planted a kiss on Reagan's cheek and leaned over to take a whiff of the wax warmer.

"Smells like Mom's bakery. Are you sure these are candles and not her cinnamon buns?"

"That's what we're going for. Cinnamon Bun Surprise," Reagan said, snuggling into his side. She'd operated a successful candle business with her mother and sister for years before moving to Jewel River. Now she owned R. Mayer Chocolates, a gourmet chocolate store in town.

Brooke couldn't have picked a better bride for her brother. And while she loved that they were so affectionate, it always brought a pang to her chest. She'd had that kind of love once. And she wouldn't have it again.

"I'm surprised Dean isn't staying at his dad's house." Brooke craned her neck to check on the girls. As if on cue, they scampered back into the dining room. Each grabbed one of Marc's legs, pulling on his jeans to pick them up.

"Girls, leave Uncle Marc alone. He's played with you since we got here." She wiped her hands with a paper towel. "Come on. It's time to settle down. I'm putting on a Christmas movie for you."

The girls were infatuated with Christmas cartoons. She found the remote and helped the girls get settled on the couch. Then she unfolded a red-and-green-plaid throw blanket and tucked it over their legs.

"There. Cozy?" She bopped the tips of each of their noses with her index finger and gave them both a smile.

"Yes, Mama." They held their arms out for a hug. She hugged them and straightened. "I'm helping Auntie Reagan with the candles, so come get me if you need anything, okay?"

"Okay."

She returned to the dining room, keeping an eye on the twins as she took a seat. Both girls had their eyes glued to the screen. Reagan was placing metal clips on top of the jars to keep the wicks in place. "Ready to fill these?"

"Yep." Brooke followed her instructions and carefully filled each jar. Then she stepped back and admired their handiwork. The candles looked great. In a day or two, after they'd cooled, she would apply the labels Reagan had printed for them. She couldn't wait to give them to her friends this Christmas.

"I told Dean he could stay here for as long as he wants." Marc rested his forearms on the table. "He mainly needs a place to stable Dusty."

"He's bringing his horse?" Brooke was taken aback. Why would he do that?

"He's dealing with a lot. He basically dropped everything to drive here."

What did "drop everything" mean? Before she could ask, a knock on the front door had them all turning their heads. Marc got up and hurried down the hallway.

"Looks like we finished just in time." Reagan turned off the wax warmer, while Brooke stood to pack away the other supplies. "I can drop these off after I close up tomorrow if you want."

Just one of the perks of buying the house in town. Reagan's chocolate shop, their mother's bakery and her mom's bungalow were within a few blocks of her house. Brooke had been grateful it had gone up for sale in the summer. She'd waited for the big renovations to be completed before moving out of her mom's place. Everyone told her to wait until all the projects were completed, but Brooke needed her independence.

She also needed to be able to recover from a medical emergency at home. With her girls.

The stroke had robbed her of her peace of mind. Every day she worried about having another one. If only the renovations were finished…

But she knew Reagan had spoken the truth earlier. The house would get finished at some point. Brooke would have to trust the Lord would provide what she needed.

The sound of the front door opening forced her thoughts back to where they belonged. On Dean. Poor guy was standing on the doorstep and probably terrified of losing his father. The man needed support and compassion. Her problems would have to wait.

As the door opened, Dean felt the first stirrings of hope since finding out his father—his larger-than-life dad—had collapsed from a heart attack. The light from inside the house glowed, and Marc didn't say a word, just pulled him in for a big hug.

Dean hadn't realized how much he'd needed that hug until Marc stepped back. "Come inside."

"I've got to take care of Dusty first." After getting Brenda's call yesterday, it was as if a switch inside him had flipped. It was time to make changes. He'd been living a shell of a life for over ten years.

Dean had immediately quit his job as a ranch hand. Then he'd packed his meager belongings, hitched his horse trailer to his truck, loaded Dusty in it and driven from Texas straight to the hospital in Casper. He'd called Marc on the way and had slumped in relief when Marc had insisted he stay with him and Reagan. Their ranch was forty minutes closer to the hospital than his dad's house on the other side of Jewel River.

That wasn't the main reason he wanted to stay with them, though. He had unfinished business at his childhood home. And he wasn't ready to deal with it.

"What else needs to be done?" Marc asked.

"Nothing."

"You know the way to the stables. I'll join you in a minute. Let me grab a coat."

Shivering as the cold air seeped through his unzipped jacket, Dean headed back to his truck. *Take care of Dusty. Then do the next thing. And the next.*

Before coming here, he'd stopped at the hospital. His father had been in the middle of a procedure, and the staff had advised Dean to come back in the morning.

His dad was probably hooked up to a million machines. What was going to happen with McCaffrey Construction while he recovered? If he recovered…

Dean couldn't go there. Couldn't imagine the world without his dad in it.

The drive to the stables took all of two minutes. As his boots hit the gravel, the reality of what he was facing smacked him.

Dad might die. Even if he survived, Dean would likely be in town for a while. While he appreciated Marc and Reagan's hospitality, he didn't want to overstay his welcome. At some point, he'd have to move—temporarily—into Dad's place. The furniture and appliances had been updated, but everything else, except the basement, was the way he'd left it as a twenty-one-year-old college dropout.

He only had bad memories of that time in his life. He

hadn't dealt with them, and he didn't want to. That was just one of the reasons he hadn't come back all that often during the past ten years.

As he stepped out of the truck, the reality of his situation overwhelmed him. *God, You aren't going to let him die, are You?*

During the long drive here, Dean had scrambled to remember every detail of the last time he'd been with his father. Their last phone conversation. The last text messages. Would there be any more? His father's health teetered on the edge.

Heart attack. Open heart surgery. Triple bypass. What did it all mean?

Icy blasts burrowed under his coat collar as a familiar sense of bleakness filled him. At least this time, he had friends to count on. He was older, wiser than the night ten years ago when his life had fallen apart.

Dean strode to the door of the stables. It slid open easily, and he switched on the lights before heading down the aisle in search of an empty stall. The scent of straw and dust and manure made him feel at home. Not surprising. It had taken a job on a ranch to save him from himself.

Within minutes, he'd led Dusty out of the trailer and gotten the horse settled into a stall. He was in the middle of filling a bucket with water when Marc strode his way.

"How are you holding up?"

"About as good as can be expected." He finished watering the horse, patted his neck one more time, then headed out of the barn with Marc. "I appreciate you and Reagan letting me crash here."

"Anytime. You're like my brother."

"You're the closest thing to a brother I have. It means a lot to me." Unlike Marc, Dean didn't have siblings. Didn't have a mother, either. She'd moved away after his parents divorced, disappearing from his life altogether.

"Stay as long as you need."

"I won't impose long. Just until I find out what's happening with Dad."

"You're not imposing." Marc put his hand on Dean's shoulder. "I want you around."

His throat grew thick with emotion. They piled into Dean's truck and drove back to the house.

The velvety black sky seemed to stretch forever as they walked to the house's side entry. Inside the mudroom, Dean took off his cowboy boots and hung his coat and Stetson on a hook on the wall. After washing up, he followed Marc into the kitchen. The place smelled like cinnamon. Overhead lights spread a cheerful glow as they passed the living room, where he caught a glimpse of two cute toddlers almost asleep on the couch. Brooke's girls. He recognized them from the wedding.

A Christmas tune played from a cartoon on TV. Christmas—another thing he couldn't bear to think about at the moment. Up ahead in the dining room, Brooke and Reagan stood side by side with matching sympathetic expressions.

Reagan was the first to step forward. She gave him a brief hug. "I'm so sorry, Dean."

Then Brooke approached, and he forgot how to breathe. She'd captivated him at the wedding. How could anyone ignore her beauty? Her shiny black hair was tied back and pulled over her shoulder, and she looked up at him through enormous dark blue eyes. She had a casual style, and her figure could only be described as curvy.

As far as he could tell, she was perfect in every way.

She embraced him, and he wanted to sink into her arms for eternity. But, like all things, the hug ended too soon.

A bunch of jars took up one side of the dining table. Candles, he guessed. The cinnamon aroma grew stronger as he sat down.

"I'll put on a pot of decaf." Reagan flitted across the room toward the kitchen. "Marc, could you help me?"

He nodded and left Dean alone with Brooke, who pulled out a chair across from him at the table.

"It's a lot to take in, isn't it?" Her big eyes shimmered with compassion.

"Yeah, it is." He wiped his hand down his cheek as exhaustion took over. He'd been driving all day with only a few stops for gas and fast food.

"One minute everything's fine, and the next?" Her right shoulder lifted in a shrug. She tossed her head to the side as if to say, *What do you do?*

"Your dad has a heart attack followed by triple bypass surgery," he finished for her.

She reached over and covered his hand with hers. Her touch eased his tension. "How is he?"

"I'm not sure. He was having a procedure when I left the hospital. They wouldn't let me see him. Told me to come back in the morning."

"If you want to go back and stay there, Marc will take care of your horse." Her long eyelashes fluttered as she blinked.

Should he go back? Was that expected? He was too tired to even think straight.

"But you should probably stay here and get some sleep," she said. "Try not to worry. He's in good hands."

"How can you be sure?"

"I spent a week at the same hospital when I had my stroke. The staff knows what to do." How could she speak so calmly about it? He still couldn't wrap his brain around the fact she'd had a stroke. Brooke was so vibrant. "In the meantime, we're here for you. Whatever you need."

"Thank you." As he stared into her enormous eyes, it hit him again how much they'd both changed in the past ten years. He'd never been close to Brooke. She'd always seemed so much younger than him and Marc. She didn't anymore. "I have to ask, though. What have I ever done for you? Why would you offer to help me?"

She averted her gaze as if she wasn't sure how to answer. "Because your father means a lot to this town, and you're my brother's best friend. I understand how tough times rip your world apart like a tornado."

And there it was.

Reality.

His father did mean a lot to Jewel River. Ed McCaffrey was the guy everyone called to have their homes built, businesses refurbished, kitchens remodeled. His dad was reliable, dependable, and he excelled at everything he touched.

Basically, he was everything Dean was not. An alarming thought came to him. Would the town expect Dean to fill in at McCaffrey Construction while his dad recovered?

Those shoes were too big to fill. Always had been.

Marc returned and pulled out a chair to take a seat. "We've got you in the spare bedroom upstairs."

Reagan followed and sat, too. "I'm glad you're staying with us, Dean."

"Thank you. I appreciate it." He'd liked Reagan from the second he'd met her. She didn't have a mean bone in her body. "I'll be out of your hair soon. But it's tricky because I don't have anywhere else to keep Dusty."

"You're not in our hair," Marc said. "You and Dusty can

stay with us for as long as you want. I wish you weren't back under these circumstances, but it sure is good to see you."

Two beeps brought Reagan to her feet. Brooke followed her to the kitchen, and Dean watched them until they disappeared from view.

The emotions he'd been stuffing down since getting Brenda's call bubbled to the surface. He wasn't sure how much longer he could avoid the fear. What he needed was some time to himself.

"I'm pretty tired." He spoke the truth. He also knew he'd be awake for hours.

"Let's get you settled. Then you can have a couple of Mom's leftover doughnuts and some decaf. It will do you good."

"I can't argue with that." And he wouldn't, even if he could.

Dean forced himself to his feet and went outside to get his bags from the truck. Minutes later, he followed Marc upstairs to the guest room. Rubbed his temples with the span of one hand.

"Come down when you're ready." Marc clapped him on the shoulder and left the room.

Ready? He didn't think he'd ever be ready. The scene in the dining room had been what he'd been avoiding for a decade. A home. A life. A family. Things he couldn't—wouldn't—have.

If only he hadn't been such a hothead at twenty-one. He'd left town in a rush with get-rich-quick plans and the wrong people along for the ride. Within a year, the situation had unraveled, and one night had changed everything. He'd lost his job, his girlfriend and his self-respect.

That was why he'd started over as a ranch hand in northern Texas. And closed himself off to everything else.

"Dean, do you take cream or sugar?" Reagan yelled from the staircase.

He tilted his head back and gazed at the ceiling. They'd welcomed him into their home. Were fine with him and his horse being here indefinitely. He couldn't stay up here and avoid them, no matter how much he wanted to.

"Cream, please!" He tightened his jaw. Having to socialize with his well-meaning friends wasn't easy. He'd been a loner for ten long years. And now he had a feeling he was going to be thrust into the community, whether he wanted to be or not.

It was time to face facts. If Dad recovered, he *would* expect Dean to step in and manage the current projects. And if he didn't recover?

Dean would have to finish what he could and cancel anything that hadn't been started.

He didn't belong in Jewel River. Didn't know where he did belong, either, but it wasn't here.

In the next month or two, Dean would start over. Somewhere new. Somewhere that didn't tempt him to believe he could have the kind of life guys his age had.

He'd gotten off easy the last time his world had tipped over. His anger hadn't caused any permanent damage. But that was a blessing—and he couldn't risk a repeat.

Chapter Two

"You just asked me that, Mom." Brooke propped her cell phone between her ear and her shoulder as she opened the door to the community center on Tuesday evening. She'd dropped off the twins at her mother's house a few minutes ago. "Okay, I'll try to find out. I'm walking in now. Love you."

Her leg was bothering her today. She hadn't slept well, and the damaged muscles weren't happy about it. Most of the time, no one was able to tell she'd had a stroke. On days like this, though, her limp made it obvious to the world that something wasn't quite right.

She ended the call with her mom, tossed the phone in her purse and gingerly made her way to the tables shoved together to form a U. Marc had saved her a seat. She was pleasantly surprised at how bright the newly renovated space appeared. The walls still had the smell of fresh paint. A decorated Christmas tree stood in the corner, and imitation evergreen garlands had been strung throughout the room. Red bows tied everything together.

How she loved Christmas. Her favorite time of the year. And this year, she wanted to enjoy it again.

"I haven't been here since it reopened."

"Looks good, doesn't it?" Marc helped her out of her coat.

"Yes, it does. By the way, Mom wants me to ask you—for

the seventeenth time, I might add—if you made sure Dean was joining us for Thanksgiving." She slung her coat over the back of the folding chair, then took a seat.

Dean had been staying at Marc's ranch since Friday. While Brooke wanted him to spend Thanksgiving with them, she knew he might have plans to keep his dad company at the hospital. And shouldn't Mom be badgering Marc about it instead of her?

Mom's phone call was precisely the reason she'd moved into her new house *before* the renovations were complete. Her micromanaging ways made Brooke want to tear her hair out. Anne Young had firm ideas on how things should be done. And Brooke was finding her own way through single parenthood.

She and her mom got along best when they lived apart.

Marc groaned. "How many times can she remind me? She knows I asked him on Sunday and again yesterday. The only reason I haven't mentioned it today is because I haven't seen him. He's been at the hospital."

"How's Ed doing?" Dean had been visiting his father every day, but yesterday was the first day Ed had spoken. Apparently, he'd been heavily sedated in the ICU all weekend. She hoped things would start to get more normal for both of them.

"I didn't ask. I'm trying to give Dean space. I'll try to find out later when I get home."

Christy Moulten tapped Brooke on the shoulder. "Howdy, neighbor. It's good to see you here."

"Hi, Christy." Brooke rose slightly to give her a quick hug, then sat back down. "I love the wreath you put out. It's gorgeous. I'm still pinching myself that we're neighbors."

"Technically, you live four houses apart." Marc lifted his index finger. Smarty pants.

"We're neighbors." Brooke waved him off and turned back to Christy. She loved the woman. Christy had recently turned sixty-five, and her sons, Cade and Ty, had thrown her a big birthday party. Her Pomeranian, Tulip—a therapy dog for the nursing home—had worn a tiny party hat. The twins were obsessed with the little fluff ball.

"I wish you'd brought those babies. They get cuter by the minute."

"They're with Mom tonight. I hope she doesn't go overboard with the sugar."

Christy chuckled. "She does own a bakery. And she *is* a grandma. It's inevitable. I hope Cade and Mackenzie want children right away. The wedding will be here before we know it."

"I can't wait."

"Any news on when your bathroom will be finished?" Christy stopped by regularly, mainly to spoil the twins, and she knew all about Brooke's remodeling woes.

"No. That's kind of why I'm here tonight." Kind of? It was the only reason. Not knowing what was going to happen to her unfinished bathroom and the nonexistent ramp had been tying her in knots for the past couple of days.

Not many people truly understood why she wanted the house completely accessible for wheelchairs. Why would they? They hadn't been stuck in a hospital, barely able to move one side of their body for a week. They hadn't spent three weeks in a long-term rehab facility working tirelessly to regain their strength so they could go home to their babies.

They hadn't had their life put on hold for a month as they worried they might never recover.

And they had no comprehension of how terrifying it was that she could have another stroke at any moment. Stroke victims automatically had a higher chance of having another one. Her neurologist and Dr. South, her general practitioner here in town, had urged her to be aware of the symptoms and to manage her risk factors.

She knew the symptoms. Had memorized the risk factors. What no one told her, though, was percentages, and all her internet searches yielded no concrete numbers. How high of a chance were they talking about? Fifty percent? Seventy-five?

Her bathroom and ramp needed to be finished.

This morning she'd called Brenda, Ed's administrative assistant, for an update on what was happening with her bathroom. The news wasn't good. The subcontractors' hands were tied moving forward on the existing projects. If the materials had already been delivered, they would do the work. For everything else? They were waiting for the green light from Ed. When Brooke had asked Brenda who else could give them the green light, she hadn't gotten an answer.

Henry Zane, the building inspector, was attending the Jewel River Legacy Club meeting tonight and might have more information.

"I guess I'd better get to my seat." With a wave, Christy hustled over to her chair.

Erica Cambridge took her spot at the podium, and everyone grew quiet. Brooke had never been to one of these meetings before. She'd never had a reason to attend. Now she was curious to see what they were all about.

Clem Buckley, the steely-eyed rancher who absolutely terrified her, called everyone to rise while he led them in the Pledge of Allegiance and the Lord's Prayer.

"Welcome, everyone," Erica said as they got settled. "I know you're all busy getting ready for Thanksgiving, so I'll try to keep this as brief as possible."

She went through old business, and Cade, Clem and Marc gave updates on their committees. As the meeting wore on,

Brooke wished someone would bring up the fact that Mc-Caffrey Construction was on hold at the moment. Should she mention it? Or should she corner Henry after the meeting? She had no clue how these things worked.

"Erica?" Angela Zane, Henry's wife, held up her hand.

"Yes?" Was Brooke imagining it, or did Erica's face look pinched?

"Joey and Lindsey put together a short film for the Christmas festival. Will there be someone at the Winston a day or two ahead of time, so he can get it set up to play on a loop?"

"Yes, Dalton and I will be on hand with the volunteers the day before. I have to ask, though, is the film appropriate for children? Not too…intense? I seem to recall you mentioning, and I quote, 'extreme reindeer games where only the tough survive.'"

"Oh, no, hon. Joey scrapped that idea. This one is for the kiddos. He assured me it's a winner for every age."

Clem shook his head. "He's going to terrify the babies. I haven't seen a film of his yet that didn't involve blowing up buildings or people running for their lives."

"Clem does have a point." Erica held out her hands, palms up. "We'll need to preview it before showing it at the festival."

Angela's thumbs traveled over her phone screen. "I've got it right here. If I send it to you, can we watch it now?"

Erica hesitated. "Su-u-re."

Dalton, Erica's husband, stood and pulled down the screen at the front of the room while Erica wheeled over the audio-visual equipment.

As much as Brooke enjoyed Joey's films, she hoped this wouldn't take long. She needed answers, not a full Christmas movie.

Soon, the lights dimmed, and the movie began to play. A

fireplace with a crackling fire appeared. Then a fluffy orange cat wearing an elf hat walked past it and let out a meow. A yellow Lab with felt reindeer antlers came into view, and he too walked past the fire. Then a butterscotch-colored Angora rabbit with a red Mrs. Claus cape tied around its neck hopped past. The camera zoomed to the window, where snow fell against a night sky, then returned to the fireplace, where all three animals were lying in a row on a rug in front of the fire. The words Merry Christmas danced across the screen. And then it was over.

Her girls were going to love it. They couldn't get enough of dogs, cats or bunnies. Very cute.

"Well, I'll be." Clem shook his head in wonder. "He did it. He actually made a film with no explosions."

"I think we should have a show of hands to approve this." Erica gazed around the room. "Who's in favor?"

Everyone raised their hands.

"Great. This is going to be a terrific addition to the festival."

Angela beamed.

Erica was about to wrap up the meeting when Patrick Howard, the owner of the future service dog training center, stood. "This might not be the place to ask, but do any of you know what's happening with McCaffrey Construction while Ed's recovering?"

Relief blew through Brooke. Finally.

Henry Zane cleared his throat. "Construction can continue on the current projects, but his subcontractors don't have the supplies they need for all of them. Since Ed supervises everything himself, no one is certain what's going on. When he gets back, he'll sort it out."

"Is he expected back soon?" Patrick asked.

"Unlikely. I spoke with Dean earlier, and there's a good possibility Ed will be in Casper for at least a few more weeks."

"My dogs will be arriving in mid-January," Patrick said. "I don't know that I can wait too long."

Brooke thrust her hand in the air. "Could someone else act as supervisor in his place?"

Henry rubbed his chin and frowned. "Depends on if they're employed by McCaffrey Construction and what role in the company they already have. If he's authorized someone, then yes. I don't know if he has, though."

Brooke chewed on that information. Surely Ed had authorized someone else to handle the business in case of something like this. From all appearances, though, it wasn't likely. Now what was she supposed to do?

The meeting wrapped up, and she and Marc stood to leave.

"I'll talk to Dean about what's going on with his dad's business." Marc helped her into her coat.

"I was thinking of doing the same, but I feel selfish. He's already going through a lot. His dad's business should be the last thing on his mind."

"Acting as supervisor might give him something to focus on."

"Supervisor? Dean? But he hasn't been involved with Mc-Caffrey Construction in ten years. I don't see that happening."

"You never know." Marc shrugged.

"Henry said he'd need to be an employee and authorized to work on behalf of the company. Or did I understand that wrong?"

"You got it right. I have a feeling that won't be an issue. Ed's always wanted Dean to join the company." Marc gestured for her to head to the door. "When Dean's not at the hospital, all he does is ride Dusty around the ranch. If he's going to be in Jewel River for a while, he might welcome the distraction. He's got the experience. Worked for his dad all through high school until he moved to Texas."

"Yeah, but it's a lot to ask…" They emerged outside in the parking lot, where cold air and a star-filled sky greeted them.

"He quit everything, Brooke." Marc matched her slower pace. "Packed up his truck, quit his job. He has no immediate plans."

"How did he manage to do that?" The picture of Dean that Marc painted seemed bleak. There must not have been much keeping him in Texas.

"I don't know. But something changed him a decade ago. He's never told me what happened. But he hasn't been the same since."

"If you think him taking over as supervisor will help him through this, I'm all for it."

They shared a smile as she settled into the driver's seat of her minivan.

"It can't hurt to ask," he said.

"All he can say is no."

"Maybe *you* should ask him."

"Why me?" She blanched at the thought.

"Because you actually have a house with unfinished projects. It might motivate him to say yes."

She buckled her seat belt and looked up at him. "I don't know."

"All he can say is no, right?" he mimicked her.

She sighed. "I'll think about it."

"You can ask him at Thanksgiving. I'll make sure he's there." Then he shut the door and waved before turning away to find his truck.

Thanksgiving was two days away. Why did she feel like she'd walked right into that one?

* * *

Tuesday night, while Marc was in town for a meeting, Dean stood on the walkway of his father's house and stared at the front door. The home he'd grown up in. The one he couldn't bring himself to enter.

He spun the key ring around his finger. Again. And again.

His conversation with his father at the hospital earlier still gnawed at him. Dad had finally been able to talk coherently. Too bad the conversation had gone to one of the few places Dean wanted to avoid.

His father had asked him point-blank to oversee the current projects for McCaffrey Construction. Dean had almost said no. He'd wanted to say no. Instead, he'd changed the subject.

He felt like a loser. Like a greedy jerk.

His dad had never abandoned his dream of wanting Dean to eventually take over the company. He'd also never listened when Dean explained he wasn't the man for the job.

Yet his dad clearly thought otherwise. Why else would he have kept Dean on the employee roster? And listed him as second-in-command? And kept his name on all the bank accounts? Dean hadn't even known about all that until this afternoon.

Why did his father still give him the benefit of the doubt? He didn't deserve it.

Back when he'd been twenty-one and an expert on everything, Dean and his dad had gotten into the worst fight of their lives. He had just dropped out of the construction management undergrad program to work for his girlfriend Lia's father in Dallas. His roommate, Colin, had gone along for the ride. They'd both received huge sign-on bonuses to work on commercial building sites.

To say Dean's father had been upset was putting it lightly.

Dad had ranted about him having a perfectly good job in construction right here. He was supposed to work in Jewel River and join him in the family business. Why would he want to move to a big city and work for some girl's father when he could work for his own?

Dean had yelled that he wanted to make real money. His dad had scornfully called it a fool's errand. They'd argued at the top of their lungs for over an hour. And his father had said the words that had been seared on his brain: "One of these days, you're going to hurt someone with that temper."

To which Dean had replied, "Yeah, well, I got it from you."

He'd stuffed some of his belongings into a bag and left. Six months later, he and Lia had gone to a bar with Colin, and before closing time, he'd excused himself to use the rest-room. When he returned, he'd found Lia and Colin kissing. Furious, he'd marched out of there with her on his heels. He'd told Lia to call for a ride, but she'd buckled herself into the passenger seat and refused to get out.

All the way to her apartment, they'd shouted at each other. He could still feel the pressure of the accelerator under his foot as he pressed it harder. They kept going faster, faster…

And then the scream.

The crash.

The eerie quiet when all he could hear was the hiss of air releasing from a mangled valve. The realization that both he and Lia had somehow made it out alive had brought a relief so intense, he'd barely been able to breathe.

The police had given him a citation for reckless driving. Her father had fired him the next day.

Dean's life had turned upside down. Not knowing what to do but adamant he wasn't going back to his dad to hear *I told you so*, Dean had packed his things and found a job as a ranch hand in rural Texas. It was where he'd been ever since.

And here he was, transfixed by the house he'd grown up in, pushing away the same things he'd pushed away after the accident.

Regret. Shame. The desire for respect.

Dean placed his foot on the first porch step, then brought it right back.

He'd been home many times over the past decade. He and his father had patched up their differences and kept things civil by not mentioning him working for McCaffrey Construction. In fact, they skirted any talk about construction in general.

But that wasn't what was keeping Dean from entering the house right now. No, the issue of him working for his dad wasn't why he couldn't quite bring himself to climb the porch steps.

The basement was the problem.

For years, his dad had asked him to help him clean out the basement. Some of the boxes held childhood mementos, toys and papers. Other boxes weren't his, though. Several were his mother's. And there were a few items of hers he didn't want to see again. One in particular.

He'd stolen it from her before she'd left town for good.

Anything he found down there would only remind him how far he'd fallen short of his dreams. And he didn't need any more reminders at this point in his life.

Snow began to fall. Big flakes—showy ones—danced down. Made him think of snowball fights and sledding with his friends.

Dean let out a frustrated breath. His father didn't ask much of him. The man wanted him to join McCaffrey Construction and clean out the basement. Dean had no intention of joining the company, and he still couldn't handle tackling the basement.

Man, he was pathetic.

The snow chilled the exposed skin of his face and neck. He stared at the massive one-story home with shadowy tall pines behind it. *Nope.* Couldn't do it. Couldn't march up those steps and face the empty house. Without his father inside, it wasn't a home.

But maybe he *could* fill in as supervisor for his dad while he recovered.

There were only a handful of projects that needed to be finished. Patrick Howard's service dog training center was almost complete. Dan Bagley's pole barn would take about a week to wrap up. And then there was Brooke's house. A master bathroom and a ramp out back. A few weeks' worth of work if everything had already been ordered and delivered. And knowing his father, it had been. The man was as efficient as he was proficient. He gave everything his absolute best, and he'd taught Dean to do the same.

He strode back to his truck and started the engine. Now what? He'd been avoiding Marc and Reagan by doing what he always did—riding his horse and checking cattle. It was how he'd kept his distance from just about everyone for a decade.

Maybe it was time to change that, too.

Ty Moulten's ranch wasn't far away. He'd always been easy to be around, and he wasn't the type to smother him with sympathy. It just wasn't Ty's way.

Fifteen minutes later, Dean knocked on the front door of the ranch house.

"Dean." Ty's face broke into a smile. "Come in. Didn't expect to see you here."

A blast of warmth hit him as he entered the foyer. The sparsely decorated living room had hardwood floors, white walls and brown leather furniture. He instantly felt at home.

"Are you hungry? I was just getting around to eating. Had

to find a cow that wandered off. I've got venison stew simmering. You're welcome to have some."

For the first time in a week, he realized he was, in fact, hungry. "Sounds great."

He took off his coat and followed Ty to the eat-in kitchen, where Ty rummaged through cupboards and drawers for bowls and silverware. Soon, they were both blowing on spoons full of stew.

"This is good. Spicy."

"I add a pinch of cayenne." Ty met his gaze and grinned. "It's better that way."

How long had it been since he'd hung out with Ty? Thirteen, fourteen years? They'd grown apart while Dean was away at college. Dean *had* flown up for Zoey's funeral, but that was five or six years ago.

For the most part, Dean hadn't kept up with his old friends. Except for Marc. They always got together for at least a few hours when Dean came to town.

"It's tough, huh?" Ty asked with a compassionate glance.

"The meat?" He glanced at the stew.

"No, your dad having a heart attack."

Dean shoveled in another bite and nodded.

"What are the doctors saying?"

"Not much. They think he'll be in the hospital for a few weeks."

"I'm glad he survived. Ed's a good guy."

"He is." That was one point Dean had never questioned. His father *was* a good guy.

"When my dad died, my entire world shifted. Pete Moulten. My hero. Could do no wrong. Dead? Seemed impossible."

"That about sums up how I feel about my father."

Ty reached for the pepper shaker. "What have you been doing? I mean, here in town?"

"Riding my horse around Marc's ranch, mostly."

"It helps. Riding around my ranch keeps the pain away. I've got more miles on my horses than I do my truck. It's the only thing I had after Zoey died."

It was the only thing Dean had after the night of the accident, too. He completely understood.

"Now it's more of a habit, I guess." Ty took a drink of water. "I miss her. Miss what we were supposed to have. My dad's death was different. He had a full life. I miss him, but not like I do her."

"You loved her."

Ty had a faraway look in his eyes. "She was my whole life. And then she was gone."

At least he'd had the love of his life. Dean hadn't allowed himself to get close to any woman after Lia. Hadn't really allowed himself to get close to anyone. He couldn't say he'd even gotten that close to her, either.

Brooke's sympathetic blue eyes came to mind.

No. No way he was getting close to Brooke. He couldn't bear to fall for her and have her see what he hid from everyone—what the accident had taken from him.

What no one knew, including his father, was that the accident had fundamentally changed him. He hadn't been able to drive with a passenger in his vehicle since the crash. On the few occasions he'd tried, he'd had a full-blown panic attack.

What could he possibly offer a woman if he couldn't even drive her anywhere? If he couldn't be certain he wouldn't snap and cause another accident?

He couldn't. And he wouldn't waste a minute thinking he could have a woman like Brooke. She needed a man she could depend on. He'd never be that man.

He'd make the best of his time in Jewel River. Try to figure out what could be done for McCaffrey Construction's unfinished projects. Maybe even attempt to go through some of the boxes in Dad's basement. But as soon as his father was home and back to work, Dean was leaving town. Starting over somewhere else. Alone.

Chapter Three

❦

"I brought pies. Two pumpkin, two apple and one pecan." Carrying a stack of plastic pie containers, Brooke's mom bustled into the kitchen of Marc's house.

"How many do you think we're going to eat? We don't need a pie per person." Brooke flashed a smile as she finished wiping Megan's hands, then tossed the wet paper towel into the trash. Marc and Reagan had offered to host Thanksgiving this year, so she'd arrived early to help cook. Reagan was busy making a tablescape—whatever that was—in the dining room, and Marc was doing ranch chores. Brooke reached for the pies her mom carried. "Here, let me."

"They'll all get eaten eventually. Thanks, honey. I'll go get the other ones." Mom kissed Brooke's cheek. "Happy Thanksgiving. You look beautiful."

"Thank you, Mom." Her mother didn't toss around compliments like confetti, so she would tuck this one away to savor later.

Alice and Megan charged toward their grandma.

"Oh, I see you!" She opened her arms wide and pulled them in for hugs. Then she kissed the tops of their heads. "My sweet girls."

"Gwammy!" They bounced in excitement, arms in the air as she straightened.

"Grammy's got to bring in the other pies. I'll be right back." She turned to leave, but paused. "Is Dean here yet?"

"Marc expects him soon."

"Good." She disappeared from view.

Despite Marc's insistence that Brooke be the one to broach the subject of Dean possibly supervising the projects for McCaffrey Construction, she'd decided she wasn't going to do it. Dean might be drifting in a sea of uncertainty, but despite what Marc thought, asking him to renovate her bathroom and build her a ramp was selfish. What he needed was for his father to heal and return home, not extra work.

"Girls, I need you to get out of the kitchen." Brooke guided them out. "This oven's hot. Go get your babies, okay?"

"Babies!" Alice yelled, clapping her hands and running on chubby legs to the living room.

Megan wrapped her arms around Brooke's calf and looked up at her with a pouty face. "Up, Mama."

"In a bit, Meggie. I have to check on the turkey."

Her bottom lip plumped out. Brooke leaned over and pretended to munch on her neck. "Gobble, gobble, gobble."

She giggled and ran off to join her sister.

Brooke shook her head, smiling to herself. Their personalities were shining through more and more as each day passed. It was hard to believe they'd be two in January. She'd have to ask Reagan for tips on throwing them a party. Her sister-in-law, whom she considered one of her best friends, was the most creative person she had ever met.

The mudroom door let out a creak. Brooke gave the potatoes a stir, then quickly peeked at the turkey so she could help her mom carry in the rest of the desserts. Hopefully, she'd also brought her highly anticipated corn casserole.

"Look who I found in the driveway." Her mom practically pushed Dean into the kitchen. "You thought you could sneak away on your horse, didn't you? Not today, mister. We have too much good food, and you have to help us make a dent in it."

He held the corn casserole in his hands. Phew.

"Sorry she forced you in here." Brooke took the dish from him. "Mom's mission in life is to make sure everyone is fed."

Her mother shot her a fake glare and brushed by carrying the other pies, a plastic bag dangling from her arm. "Don't apologize for me. I know what cowboys are all about. They retreat to the barn, lose track of time, and the next thing you know, supper's cold and everyone's cranky."

She cruised out of the room, and Brooke bit the corner of her bottom lip to keep from laughing.

"It's okay if you need to check on Dusty," she said. "I'll cover for you."

"No, that's okay. I'll stay." His hands dropped to his sides. "I fed and watered him this morning."

Dean had made an effort to look nice. His scruff had been trimmed, and he wore a button-down shirt with jeans. She, too, had taken extra care with her appearance. She had on her favorite stretchy jeans and a red sweater. Her hair was actually holding the curls she'd coaxed earlier with her curling iron, and she'd applied lipstick, blush and eyeliner.

"How's your dad doing?" She pointed to the counter behind him. "Would you toss me those oven mitts?"

"He's better." He handed them to her.

"How much better? Do the doctors have a plan? I feel bad that he's stuck there on Thanksgiving."

"I do, too. When I left him earlier, he was falling asleep. I told him I'd come up again tonight. Your mom already insists she's packing him a full meal. I don't think his nurses will be pleased, but I don't know how to say no to her."

"Mom's formidable. No one can say no to her." She opened

the oven door and popped the casserole into the oven. "Did anyone say when he'd be released?"

Dean sighed, which made her think maybe she shouldn't be prying.

"He'll leave the hospital on Saturday."

That sounded promising. Maybe Ed would be back to work soon. Her goal of having the house completely renovated by Christmas *could* still happen.

"But they're sending him to a rehab center to build up his strength."

Her hope collapsed—not for her house or renovation dreams, but for Ed. And for Dean.

"I'm sorry. What rehab center is he going to?" He named the same one she'd been transferred to last year. "They're good. You don't have to worry about how he'll be treated. I spent three weeks there after my stroke."

He blinked twice as a wrinkle formed between his eyebrows. "Why did you have to stay for so long?"

"My left side was weak. At first, I couldn't lift my arm or move my leg at all. I had to do physical and occupational therapy every day for hours. The staff helped me regain my strength. It's amazing how much I took for granted before the stroke—basic things, like walking up a step or holding my babies. I'm grateful God spared me from permanent paralysis."

This time, at least. Who knew what the future held?

"I wish He would have spared you from having the stroke in the first place."

"Same here." She reached around him to open a drawer. He smelled good, like woodsy aftershave. After finding the can opener, she used the crook of her arm to slide several canned goods her way. "I'm doing everything I can to live my best life and keep moving forward."

"Your best life. I like the sound of that." He leaned against the counter and watched her open green beans, then dump them into a colander in the sink. "What's changed?"

"I'm mindful of my health. I keep a running list of doctor's orders in my head at all times." She lowered her voice to mimic the doctor. "Don't let yourself get too tired. Drink a lot of water. Rest often. Eat a balanced, healthy diet. Be aware of the signs of stroke."

His frown deepened. "You mean you could have another one?"

Growing serious, she nodded and kept her gaze on the colander as she shook it.

"I'm at an increased risk. I'll always be." She reached up for a baking dish. After greasing it, she stirred together all the ingredients for the green bean casserole. "I hope to never be a patient at the rehab center again. If I didn't have the girls, it wouldn't be such a big deal, but being separated from them?" She shook her head in defiance. "No. Not going through that again."

"Happy Thanksgiving!" Marc's deep voice bellowed from the mudroom. Then he entered the kitchen and grinned at Dean. "You made it."

"I'm here."

"Let me get cleaned up, and we can find out what the ladies need help with."

"Marc?" Mom called from the other room.

"Yes, Mother?"

"This leaf is stuck. The pegs aren't lining up correctly."

"Think you can help them with it?" Marc asked Dean.

"Yeah, go get changed. I've got it."

Marc hurried away, and Dean pointed his thumb to the dining room. "I'll go see if I can help."

Brooke nodded. Had she overshared? It wasn't like she

went around giving everyone her sob story. The people in Jewel River already knew it. News and gossip traveled fast in these parts. So why had she confided in him?

His dad is in the same rehab center you spent so much time in. It's normal to open up about your own experience there. Don't beat yourself up. It's not a secret.

Dean deserved a relaxing Thanksgiving. From this point on, she wouldn't mention anything that would remind him his dad had a long road to recovery ahead.

Just how long of a road would it be, though? She wished she'd asked.

"Brooke?" her mom yelled.

"What?"

"How long until the turkey is done?"

"We should be ready to eat in about an hour."

"Good. That will give us time to fill out our thankful leaves."

She rotated the corn casserole and jammed the green bean casserole next to it. It just fit. Then she washed her hands and went to check on the twins. She found them in the dining room. Reagan held Alice on her hip, and Dean was crouching with his hand outstretched to take Megan's stuffed dog. Meggie giggled as he brought it to his chest.

"This is a good puppy, isn't it?" His brown eyes crinkled in the corners. He cradled the dog, and Megan clapped her hands, clearly delighted. "What's the puppy's name?"

"Booboo." Megan turned away to grab a small blanket. "Cold."

"Booboo's cold?" He wrapped the puppy in the blanket. "We'd better warm him up. That's better."

Brooke hung back in the archway as unexpected emotions rose. She'd watched Marc with the girls since the day they were born. He treated them like any proud uncle would.

But Dean…he reminded her of Ross. Which, in turn, tightened a vise around her chest. The girls didn't have a father. If Ross had lived, they'd have one who loved them dearly. But he hadn't lived.

Her babies were facing a lifetime with no daddy. Was she making the right choice by refusing to even consider dating again?

While Dean had wished God had spared her from having the stroke, she personally wished God had spared her from losing Ross. For months now, she'd found herself forgetting things about him she'd clung to so tightly after his death. The way he smiled. His goofy laugh. Looking at a photo on her phone wasn't the same.

Her memories of Ross were fading more rapidly each day. How long would it be until she forgot him altogether?

She bunched her hands into fists.

Don't think about it. Don't dwell on the past. Enjoy this moment.

She'd been giving herself the same advice for well over a year, but sometimes it was hard.

The sound of water boiling over made her rush back to the kitchen. The potatoes were overflowing. She turned down the burner and mopped up the spill bubbling around the pot as best as she could.

"Here, let me." Dean had followed her. He took the dish towel from her hand and dabbed at the spills. "Don't want you to burn yourself."

"Thanks." His presence, or maybe his thoughtfulness, made her tummy swirl. It certainly wasn't hunger causing it. She'd been snacking all day.

"Your girls are cute." He stepped back, still holding the dish towel.

"Thank you." She wholeheartedly agreed. They were adorable, and yes, she knew she was biased. "Here, I'll take that." She took the cloth from him and hung it over the dishwasher handle to dry.

"I wish my dad was home." Dean blew out a melancholy breath.

"I wish he was, too."

"He didn't even qualify for outpatient care. I pushed for it, but apparently, Jewel River is too far from treatment centers for it to be feasible. The rehab center you were in—the one Dad's going to—you said it's good. Do you think he'll make a full recovery there?"

The change in subject startled her, but as she looked into his worried eyes, she was thankful he'd asked.

"Yes, I do believe he'll recover there. He's made it this far—the heart attack, triple bypass surgery. He's strong. He just needs a reason to work hard. I was motivated by the thought of returning home to my girls. They were babies, only three months old, when I had my stroke. To be separated from them for even a day was painful, and I was in Casper for a full month."

"Who took care of them?"

"Reagan and Marc, mostly. Mom stayed with me the first week when I was in the hospital. When I transferred to the rehab center, she visited most afternoons and helped out with the twins at night. I hadn't even met Reagan when she offered to help babysit. To think she would do that—sacrifice so much time to take care of a stranger's babies—I'll forever be in her debt."

The sound of voices made her turn.

"Do you have a gravy recipe in your family?" Mom was asking Reagan as they entered the kitchen. "It's one thing I've never mastered."

"My dad told me he adds some of the starchy potato water to the turkey drippings. Beyond that, I'm clueless."

"Potato water. Hmm…"

Brooke met Dean's gaze, and they both chuckled.

"What's so funny?" her mom asked, smiling.

"You and your gravy secrets."

"Laugh all you want, but it's not going to distract me from the fact you both need to fill out your thankful leaves." Mom thrust a stack of leaves cut out of construction paper at Brooke. "Pens are in the junk drawer. We'll be reading them out loud during supper."

Dean leaned close and whispered, "What's a thankful leaf?"

"You write something you're grateful for on it. Then we take turns sharing. If you don't want to—"

"No, no. I'll do it."

She looked into his eyes, and for the first time since she'd seen him since Friday, she saw signs of life. He appeared younger, more optimistic.

What a handsome man. And nice. Plus, the patience he'd shown Megan? He was good with kids.

With more force than necessary, she yanked open the junk drawer, found two pens and handed him one. She shouldn't be thinking along those lines. Shouldn't be noticing Dean as anything but Marc's best friend.

Truth be told, she wanted to be Dean's friend, too.

Just friends, though. If they spent too much time together, her heart would zoom way past friendship. She'd better play it safe. She had plenty to be thankful for. Letting her lonely side push her into wanting more—on Thanksgiving, no less— would only lead to trouble.

This was what he'd been missing. A big family meal with a chandelier twinkling above the dining table, empty dessert plates holding crumbs, good conversation, the occasional burst of laughter and blessings scrawled on paper leaves. Dean's thankful leaf had been easy to fill out. Dad was alive.

He couldn't stop staring at Brooke sitting across from him. One of the twins had fallen asleep on her lap. The other was sleeping on Reagan's lap.

The decision he'd made this morning had been the right one. When he'd stopped by the hospital earlier, his father had spelled out what still needed to be addressed on the construction projects. At first, Dean had mentally pulled away. But as he'd watched his father struggling to remember where the materials for Patrick Howard's kennel room were and what installer had agreed to lay the tile for Brooke's bathroom, Dean had realized how important it was that the work get finished.

McCaffrey Construction was Ed's life's work. And Dean knew that if his father didn't have to worry about the projects being left unfinished, he'd be able to fully focus on his recovery. The doctors wanted to keep Ed's stress to a minimum.

So he'd patted Dad's hand and said, "Leave everything to me. I'll handle it."

The tightness in his dad's face had instantly released. Of course, a minute later, he'd commanded Dean to take notes. Dean had diligently typed everything into his phone as his father barked orders. He figured he'd call Brenda tomorrow for more information, even though it was a long holiday weekend.

"More coffee, Dean?" Anne smiled as she approached with the coffeepot. She seemed to be around the same age as his dad. An attractive woman who got things done. And a first-class baker. Those pies had been delicious.

"Sure, why not?" He thanked her after she poured. Brooke tilted her head and watched him with a thoughtful expression. What was she thinking? Why was she looking at him like that?

Beautiful *and* kind. No wonder he couldn't stop staring at her. He'd thought about her many times since Marc and Reagan's wedding and too often to count since rolling into town last Friday.

A blast of warmth heated his core, and he had a sudden urge to excuse himself to the stables and saddle up Dusty.

"I think the game's about to start." Marc pushed away from the table. "I'll turn it on."

"Ugh." Brooke pretended to gag. "Do we have to watch football?"

"I can't believe you're saying that." Marc looked stricken. "Of course we're watching football. It's Thanksgiving. We eat turkey. We count our blessings. And we watch the Cowboys."

"Watch them lose, you mean." Anne pretended to brush off one of her shoulders.

"Oh, I see we're starting the smack talk early, Mom." Marc followed Anne out of the room as they argued about the upcoming game.

"I'm going to run the dishwasher." Reagan handed the twin she was holding to Dean. "Do you mind holding Megan?"

"Um, sure." He opened his arms to take the child. As her warm body, heavy with sleep, nestled into his chest, he stilled. He'd held plenty of small animals. Calves, dogs, injured fawns, you name it. But a tiny human? Practically a baby?

He hadn't held one of those before. And he found that he liked it.

"I can put them in their cribs to nap if you don't want to hold her," Brooke said.

"No, I don't mind." This was the perfect time to bring up her renovation. But he hadn't thought through other logistics.

Like the fact he was going to be in Jewel River through the holidays and maybe longer. He'd need to move out of Marc's spare bedroom and into Dad's house.

A shiver rippled down his back at the thought. All those boxes in the basement sitting there, waiting for him to sort through them. And now he wouldn't have an excuse to avoid them.

"I know my dad was still working on your house when he had the heart attack," Dean said. "I'm sure you must be wondering what's happening with the renovations."

Her cheeks flushed, and she gave a slight nod. "It's crossed my mind. But Ed's health is all that matters. My house can wait."

Her unselfish attitude bolstered his confidence. He was doing the right thing.

"This might sound out there, but Dad has always kept me on as an employee. Although I haven't worked for him in over ten years, he named me second-in-command. I have the authority to act in his place."

Her eyelashes blinked wide, and her pretty blue eyes glistened with hope.

"He's going to be in the rehab center for about a month. Could be longer. This morning I told him I'd supervise the current projects."

"Really? That's great!" She let out a dreamy sigh. "My goal was to have all the renovations done by Christmas."

"I'll do my best to make that happen."

"And after they're done?" A crinkle appeared above the bridge of her nose.

"What do you mean?"

"What will you do then?"

"When Dad's ready to come back to work, I'll be moving on."

"Where will you go?"

Good question. If he didn't have a sleeping toddler on his lap, he'd stand. Pace. Instead, he stretched his head side to side to work out the kinks in his neck.

"I don't know yet. Did Marc tell you I quit my job?"

"He did."

"I'm not sure what my future holds. Can't think that far ahead right now. I'll handle Dad's business and try my best to deal with all the junk in the basement, and—"

"What do you mean? What junk in the basement?"

Why had he mentioned it? He should have kept his mouth shut.

"Dad's been bugging me for years to help him clean out the basement. A lot of the boxes are mine, but I know there's other stuff down there, too. I told him to rent a dumpster and toss it all, but he's worried there are things down there I'll want."

"I can help you with it. If you want help, that is."

The idea immediately tempted him. Having Brooke there would make the process less stressful.

But then she'd see all his silly childhood keepsakes. She might unbox the things his mother had left behind before she'd moved out for good.

So what? Maybe he *was* ready to tackle the boxes in the basement. He'd get it over with, and it wouldn't hang over his head anymore.

"How long do you think it will take you to finish my house?" Brooke asked.

"I don't know. I'll have to come over and see for myself. I'm calling Brenda tomorrow to go over all the projects that are still unfinished."

"Stop by anytime. In fact, why don't you come over on Saturday? I could use an extra set of hands to set up my Christmas tree, and I hate asking Marc for help with everything, especially now that Reagan's pregnant."

Helping this beautiful woman set up a Christmas tree should be a hard no. And yet he couldn't stop himself from agreeing. "Okay. Would morning work? Or I can stop by later."

"Morning would be great."

One thing his father had mentioned about her house renovation kept nagging at him.

"I know you said you could have another stroke. Is that why you're making everything wheelchair accessible?"

She nodded.

"Do the doctors think you'll have one soon?"

"I could have one at any time, or I could live the rest of my life without having another stroke. I'm being proactive. I spent weeks in the rehab center. Like your father, outpatient care wasn't an option for me." She smoothed the baby's hair as she slept. "I want to be prepared for whatever happens, including the possibility of needing a wheelchair."

He took a sip of coffee as more questions piled up. A remodeling job of her scope didn't come cheap. How could she afford it all?

"My husband was raised by his older uncle. When the man died, Ross inherited his entire estate." She stared off toward the window. Had she read his mind? "After Ross died, it all went to me. Until recently, I didn't appreciate what it meant to have those funds available. In my mind, the best way to use the money is to get my affairs in order, starting with my house. We never know what a new day might bring."

He couldn't argue with that. Still, it seemed like overkill to remodel an entire home for an emergency that might never happen.

Brooke folded the paper napkin next to her dessert plate.

"Let me know when you want to start going through the basement. I have a lot of people willing to help me with the twins. And I'm good at organizing."

It would be dumb to agree to spend more time with her. He liked her too much already. He should turn down her offer, but he needed moral support. "I could use the help."

Her radiant face flared heat up his neck. He definitely should have said no.

"Looks like I'll be staying in town for a while," he said. "I'll move my stuff over to Dad's place tomorrow."

"You can't stay there. It's too far away. It tacks on an extra forty minutes to get to the hospital. Are you sure you won't stay here?"

"I've taken advantage of Marc's hospitality long enough."

Her eyebrows drew together. "You should consider moving into Reagan's house in town. It's furnished and empty at the moment. Her renter didn't renew the lease. It's close to Ed's office. And it's only a few blocks from my house."

Only a few blocks away from Brooke? He liked the sound of that.

"I'll bunk at Dad's for now." He'd have to leave Dusty here, though. His father didn't have a barn for a horse.

"You could board Dusty at Moulten Stables. It's all of two minutes from Reagan's place. That way you could ride him whenever you felt like it."

Two minutes away from Dusty? Maybe he should stay in Reagan's house. He'd pay rent, of course. It would be convenient and give him privacy. Save him from being alone in his childhood home, surrounded by memories he'd rather avoid.

"Moulten Stables? Does Ty own it?"

"Cade. He opened the horse boarding business in September. It's right outside town." Brooke cuddled the child closer. "When Reagan comes back in, I'll mention it to her."

"Mention what?" Reagan appeared with another pie, which she set on the table. Dean couldn't eat another bite, yet his mouth watered just looking at it.

"The possibility of Dean staying at your house in town. He's going to supervise the projects for McCaffrey Construction until Ed is cleared to come back to work."

"You are? That's wonderful. You're helping so many people." Reagan appeared to be on the verge of tears even though she was smiling. "Please stay in my house. I'll go grab the keys. It's clean and ready whenever you want to go over there. But don't get the wrong impression—I'm not trying to get you out of here. You're welcome to stay as long as you want."

Dean glanced from Brooke to Reagan and back to Brooke. That was resolved quickly.

"Looks like I'm moving into town tomorrow. Thank you."

"We'll have to set up two Christmas trees," Brooke said. "One for you, and one for me."

He didn't bother telling her he always skipped Christmas decorating. His cabin in Texas had been smaller than a matchbox, and he hadn't had much Christmas spirit in years, anyhow.

Something told him this Christmas was going to be different, though. And his heartbeat quickened at the thought. All because of the beautiful single mom sitting across from him.

Chapter Four

Under no circumstances could he consider moving to Jewel River permanently. Mainly because Dean had never told his father about the accident and what it had done to him. He didn't deserve to be a partner at McCaffrey Construction.

Moving here would leave him exposed. It wouldn't take long for people to catch on to the fact he never drove with anyone in his vehicle. They'd want to know why.

He couldn't share his reasons. Too embarrassing. Wished he could strike that night—that entire year—from his memory altogether.

As he drove down Center Street on Friday morning, he took in the town's Christmas decorations. Wreaths hung from the front doors of the local businesses. Garland had been wrapped around the lampposts and topped with red bows. Large planters held small pine trees wound with white twinkle lights. He'd driven through Jewel River at Christmas a few times since moving to Texas, but he'd never really noticed how much effort the residents put into making it inviting, like a scene out of a holiday movie.

Dean glanced at the rearview mirror to check the horse trailer. Still there. Same as it had been every time he'd checked since loading Dusty in it at Marc's ranch. He'd called Cade Moulten earlier about renting a stall at Moulten Stables. Cade had instructed him to bring the horse over whenever was convenient—and now was the time.

While Marc and Reagan had been kind and welcoming, he was used to living alone. He needed space. Lots of space. And quiet.

Still, he appreciated how his living arrangements had fallen into place due to the generosity of his friends.

God, I'm humbled at how You've looked out for me. Thank You.

Last night, Reagan had handed him the key to her house and texted him the address. Not because she wanted him to leave. She understood, without him having to go into details, that he needed privacy.

He'd unload his stuff there after getting Dusty settled. At some point this weekend, he should probably drive out to his dad's place and actually enter his childhood home. And tomorrow morning, he'd pay Brooke a visit. Anticipation made him smile as he thought about finishing her remodeling projects. They were the easy part. Clearing out Dad's basement was the hard part. It meant he had to go down there and tackle the mess. With her help, of course.

Maybe that was the real reason his internal warning system was waving red flags about Jewel River.

Brooke.

Finishing her house. Cleaning out the basement together. Helping her put up a tree for Christmas.

All of the above appealed to him. But he couldn't go and do something stupid like get close to her. She didn't know his secrets. And he didn't plan on sharing them.

Before long, Dean pulled into Moulten Stables. He parked in front of the barn. Out on the gravel, he studied the structure. What a beauty. He made his way inside and followed the signs pointing to the office. A tall, muscular man stepped out from an empty stall. He wore jeans, a sweatshirt and an unzipped coat. Held a pitchfork.

"Trent?" Dean hadn't seen his old classmate since high school graduation.

"Dean." Trent's face broke into a wide grin. He propped the pitchfork against the wall and held out his hand, which Dean shook. Trent was taller than him, and he had short, tousled brown hair, a day's worth of scruff and an open smile. "Good to see you. Cade mentioned you'd be stopping by. I'm the manager here. Moved back in late August."

"I thought you were living down south."

"I was. When Cade called this summer, it must have been God's timing. I was ready for a new adventure. I heard about your dad. Hope he's doing better."

"He is. They're getting ready to move him to a rehab center in Casper. He'll be there for a month or so."

"You're sticking around here while he recovers?" Trent angled his chin and watched him thoughtfully.

"I am." He didn't want to get into details about why he quit his job. At some point, he'd have to figure out what he was going to do with his life. Today wasn't that day. It could wait until after Dad returned home. "Cade mentioned you had a couple of stalls available."

"We sure do. Why don't you put your horse in the paddock out back? Then I'll take you around."

Dean followed his directions. The crisp air refreshed him, and Dusty seemed to enjoy it, too. The horse snorted and tossed his mane when Dean led him into the paddock. About a dozen horses grazed in the adjacent pasture. He spent extra time with Dusty before returning to the barn.

"Ready?" Trent gestured to the aisle. Dean strolled next to him as he listed all the features and answered his ques-

tions. Then they checked out the open stalls, and Dean selected the one he wanted for Dusty.

"You've got some impressive horseflesh out in the pasture,"
Dean said. "I can see why you'd want to manage this place."

"Like I said, I was ready to move on, and I'm happy with
my decision." Back in the office, Trent nodded for him to
take a seat across from him at the desk. He slid a packet of
forms his way. "Exceptional horses. Top-notch facility. We
have riding trails leading to the wooded part of the property.
You can explore them whenever you want. I just need you to
sign these forms and put down a deposit."

Dean skimmed the forms before signing them. Then he
opened his wallet and handed Trent his debit card. "I'll check
out the trails soon, but I have other stuff to take care of
today."

"I know you've got a lot going on." Trent grew serious. "If
you can't be here, I'll take care of your horse. Text me anytime."

"That would help me out a lot. His name is Dusty. I should
be able to take care of him most days. There might be a time
or two, though, when I can't. But I wouldn't want to pull you
away from time with your family."

Trent laughed. "No family. Just me in that big old house
across the road."

For whatever reason, the fact Trent was still single brightened his mood. With Cade engaged and Marc happily married, Dean had been getting a funny feeling, but with Ty
and Trent still single, he could embrace his bachelor lifestyle without being embarrassed. He wasn't the only one
without a partner.

Ty had a good reason, though. He'd lost Zoey. And Trent
might be dating someone, or at least interested in dating
someone. Hopefully not Brooke.

He wondered why he'd had that thought.

"I'd better get going." Dean rose. "Thanks again for everything. It's good to see you."

"We'll have to get together and watch some football or grab a burger." Trent accompanied him out of the office to the main door.

"Or both. Sounds good to me."

With his top priority taken care of, Dean drove to the address Reagan had texted him. As he climbed the porch steps, he noticed two large plastic bins and an artificial tree in a box near the door. The top bin had an envelope with his name. He slipped it into his coat pocket, then unlocked the door and stepped inside.

The cold interior did nothing to dampen the warm, inviting atmosphere. Hardwood floors ran throughout, and the living room had a fireplace and plenty of windows. He ambled through the kitchen, then continued to the bedrooms. The main bedroom had an attached bathroom. It reminded him of a cozy cottage. Muted neutral tones on the walls, in the furniture and in the decorations made it feel homey.

After turning up the thermostat, Dean went back outside. As he opened the tailgate to unload his belongings, he sized up the neighborhood. The street was lined with small bungalows similar to this one, and most of the porches were decked out with Christmas lights. He placed his bags in the driveway and slammed the tailgate shut. Taking two trips, he hauled everything to the main bedroom to deal with later.

Now what? Should he unpack his clothes? Buy a few groceries? Or crash on the couch for a while to clear his head?

He *could* head over to Brooke's a day early. *Don't even think about it.* Maybe he should drive to Casper. See how Dad was doing. Last night he'd smuggled in the leftovers Anne had packed.

Dad had been sleeping when he arrived, but he'd woken immediately. They'd talked for about an hour, with Dad sampling a few bites of everything, including the pie. Dean had given him a hug and told him not to worry. He'd assured his father he'd handle whatever came up at McCaffrey Construction until he came home.

The optimistic gleam in his father's eyes hadn't escaped his notice. At some point, Dad would pressure him to stay, to join the business.

Dean didn't deserve it. Had never deserved it.

How could the man still have so much faith in him? After all the mistakes he'd made?

His father didn't know about his biggest mistake, though. The accident.

Dean wasn't in the mood to unpack. Rubbing his hands together, he remembered the envelope from the bins on the porch. He took it out of his pocket and read it. Erica Cambridge, Reagan's sister, had dropped off Christmas decorations in case he needed some.

He'd met Erica at Marc's wedding, and it didn't surprise him she would drop off decorations. The sisters clearly shared the generosity gene. He went to the porch and hauled the bins inside even though decorating for Christmas was the last thing on his mind.

Sighing, he thought of Brooke and her telling him that they should set up two trees—one at her place and one at his. Spending too much time with her would only make him want to stay. What kind of future could he possibly have here? He wasn't worthy of the kind of life people his age enjoyed. He'd had it all at twenty-one, and he'd blown it.

This cozy cottage was a temporary place to stay. Like Jewel River itself.

When his dad recovered, Dean would leave. Get back to the solitary life that suited him just fine.

Brooke wiped a warm washcloth over Megan's face Saturday morning. Had she gotten all the syrup from the pancakes? She gave her chin another wipe as Megan shook her head and cried out in protest. Alice banged her kiddie fork on the high chair tray next to her twin's. A few tiny bites of sausage Brooke had cut up earlier flew into the air and landed on the floor. Times like these made her long for a dog. It would make quick work of the messes on the floor after each meal.

"You're next, sister," Brooke muttered. She unstrapped Megan and set her on the floor, then turned to Alice. "Okay, let's get you cleaned up."

"No, no, no!" She threw the baby fork, narrowly missing Brooke's shoulder.

"That's enough of that, Alice. We do not throw our silverware." Brooke reached for the other warm washcloth she'd prepared. The twins were getting more outspoken and headstrong every day. Lately, she'd been overwhelmed and doubting her ability to raise them on her own.

Was she disciplining them enough? Too much?

Alice whined as Brooke wiped her face and hands. She cleaned her up as quickly as possible and set her down to join Megan. While the girls toddled off to the open-concept living room and dumped out a basket of toys, she wiped down their high chair trays and loaded the dishwasher.

She would not pressure Dean to rush her projects. Nor would she get her hopes up that they'd be done by Christmas. She'd simply be grateful he was willing to supervise the bathroom and ramp. But, oh, how she'd hoped everything would be done before Christmas.

When would he stop by? They'd agreed he'd come over

this morning, but did that mean early? Late? She wished they had specified a time. At least she'd been able to shower and put on a little makeup before the girls woke. Now that they'd eaten, she needed to change them out of their pajamas. But first...coffee.

She reached for the cup she'd poured earlier, took a sip and frowned. *Blech.* Cold. She popped it into the microwave, leaning against the counter while it warmed.

Yesterday, while the twins napped, she'd gotten out all of her Christmas decorations from the detached garage. She hadn't attempted to wrestle the giant box with the tree inside, though. It still sat on the shelf in the garage, where it would stay until Dean arrived.

Maybe he'd be too busy to help her set it up. Maybe he was having second thoughts about everything they'd discussed. What if he took one look at the gutted bathroom, shook his head and told her he hadn't realized it needed so much work? That he was sorry, but he couldn't do it?

And what about the ramp? Who knew how long that would take?

The microwave beeped, and she grabbed the mug, wincing as the hot steam singed her fingers. She set it on the counter. Looked like she wasn't having coffee first after all.

"Meggie, Alice, let's get dressed."

"No!" one of them yelled. Probably Alice. She tended to voice her opinion more readily.

Closing her eyes, Brooke said a silent prayer. *God, give me patience.* She hoped God didn't get tired of hearing from her, because she'd been saying that prayer an awful lot lately.

She went to the living room and picked up Alice, who began shouting and kicking as she carried her to the twins' bedroom.

"Stop kicking. You need to get out of your pajamas. We

all get dressed. Every day. See? I'm wearing a sweater and jeans."

"No!" Alice twisted to avoid the changing table, but Brooke got her up there. She hummed a song and made quick work of changing her diaper and putting on tiny leggings and a matching sweater. Then she brushed her hair, kissed the top of her head and set her on the carpet.

She repeated the process with Megan, and by the time she returned to the kitchen, her coffee had grown cold once more. She sighed. Back into the microwave.

At least the girls were happy again. They were giggling and rolling around on the rug in the living room. She savored the sounds. Toddler giggles should be bottled.

Just as she was taking out the coffee mug from the microwave, the doorbell chimed.

Her heartbeat thumped in her chest. Dean.

After a quick sip—not too hot this time—she hurried to the front door. At the sight of him standing there, she inwardly swooned. He looked as handsome as ever in jeans, a sweatshirt and an unzipped winter coat. He smiled, and the brooding air that always seemed to surround him vanished.

"Come in." She held the door open and waited for him to enter before closing it once more. "Want a cup of coffee?"

"I'd better not." His brown eyes shimmered with playfulness. "Already had two cups."

"Two barely get me started. I need a full pot."

"I get that. You have twins."

"True."

They shared a long, understanding—possibly even flirty—glance. Brooke finally pried her gaze away. The pitter-patter of little footsteps came closer. Soon, two sets of arms wrapped around her legs.

"Hey, girls. How are you?" He crouched to their level, and they hid behind her legs.

"I guess they're shy this morning." She pointed down the hall. "Let's get out of the entryway. Come on. I'll take you to my bathroom."

As soon as she began walking, the twins disengaged from her legs and flanked Dean. They did a combination of walking and hopping down the hall on either side of him. Brooke flipped on her bedroom light, then paused in the doorway of the bathroom. Dean stood next to her. She was all too aware of his presence, and the woodsy scent of his aftershave made her want to lean in closer. Instead, she held herself rigid.

It had been ages since she'd been attracted to a man, and clearly, she needed to nip whatever this was in the bud.

"As you can see, it needs a lot of work." *Please don't tell me it's in worse shape than you expected.*

"It's in better shape than I expected." *Yes.* He stepped inside. The walls had been stripped of Sheetrock, and the wiring and plumbing were new. He touched the pipes sticking out of the walls and stared at the ceiling. "Plumbing is ready. Are the electrical outlets where you want them?"

"They are. The electrician installed a few extra, too."

"Good. I looked over the blueprints yesterday. Dad already ordered everything. It's sitting in the company's storage shed. On Monday morning, I'll call a crew about coming here to install the cement board for the shower and the Sheetrock for the walls. It will take several days to mud, sand and paint everything. Then we'll install the shower tray, tile, toilet, vanity, mirrors and lights."

"Did Ed tell you I want grab bars installed?"

"Yes, and I'll put in some blocking for additional strength."

"I'll need the ramp built out back, too."

"Show me where the ramp is going."

Brooke backed up, almost knocking over Alice. She bent to lift the girl and held out her other arm for Megan. Then she slowly straightened with a twin on each hip.

"Whoa. How'd you do that?" Dean's wide eyes made her chuckle.

"A lot of practice, right girls?" They snuggled closer with their cheeks on her shoulders and stared at Dean. "The dining area off the kitchen has a door leading to the backyard and driveway. There's a small porch with steps there currently." She carried the twins out of the bedroom with Dean right behind her. The girls shifted to watch him as she continued to the kitchen, stopping near the back door.

"Hmm…may I?" Dean gestured to the door handle. Brooke nodded. He stood on the porch and surveyed the area, then came back inside. "Looks like we'll have to tear out the porch and install new posts for the ramp. Before we can dig post-holes, we'll need to have the utilities out here to mark where their lines are buried. Since it's almost December, I wouldn't be surprised if the weather will play a factor."

None of that sounded promising.

"As for the bathroom, I estimate it will take about three weeks."

"Only three weeks? That's wonderful." The bathroom would be finished in time for Christmas. She could start off the new year secure in the knowledge that the inside of the house was prepared for whatever came her way.

What if something bad came her way, though? She might be able to handle it in terms of being prepared at home, but what about mentally? Emotionally?

She needed the ramp. Needed the security it would give her. While she wanted to convince Dean how important it was that everything get finished—soon—she refrained. He was doing her a big favor. And he didn't owe her anything.

"I'll do my best to get the ramp done, too, Brooke."

Was she that transparent?

"I appreciate it. You're going through a lot, so if things take longer, I understand." She would try to be patient.

He stared at her with an expression she couldn't decipher. Heat blasted her cheeks. And she wished she still had the mug of coffee in her hands, for an excuse to look at anything besides him. A commercial from the television played "Jingle Bells."

The Christmas tree. She'd almost forgotten. "Any chance you're still willing to help me set up my Christmas tree?"

"Sure." He glanced around the space. "Where is it?"

"The box is in the garage. Bottom shelf. It's heavy, so if you don't want to—" A cold breeze alerted her he'd already gone outside and was down the porch steps. A few minutes later, he carried the large box inside.

"Follow me." Brooke crossed into the living room, not daring to look back as he hauled the box. He was one strong cowboy. It reminded her she'd been married to a strong soldier. If she had a type, both muscular men would fit it. She pointed to an empty spot near the corner, so it would be more out of the way. "Over there."

"You don't want it in front of the window?"

The large picture window overlooked the backyard. "Will it stick out too much? With the girls running everywhere, I don't know if it's wise."

"Good point." He set down the box and rubbed his chin. "The corner will work."

"What dat?" Megan pointed to the box. Alice stood next to her.

"It's our Christmas tree."

"Ooh, twee!" Alice clapped her hands.

"Mr. Dean is going to help us put it up, and then we'll decorate it later."

They turned to each other with their mouths in big Os.

"I think they like that idea." Dean grinned.

"I think you're right."

He moved the box to the corner and began unpacking it. Brooke had only used it once. It had been in storage for two years. She hoped the lights still worked.

Dean assembled the sections together in record time. When he plugged it in, all the lights worked.

"Ooh!" The girls gawked at it.

"I can fluff the branches later." Brooke dragged the empty box out of the way.

"We can get it done now," Dean said. "I don't mind helping."

She turned away at the sudden emotion his words brought up. His kindness kept poking at dormant things inside her. Things she believed she'd lost forever.

The desire to have a partner, to be able to rely on him for help—she wasn't certain she wanted those feelings back, because they only reminded her what she couldn't have. A husband, more children. Not with her health problems. She would not put a man through that stress, and she wouldn't put herself through another pregnancy. Her girls were too important to take that risk.

"No, that's okay." She forced a tight smile on her face. "You're busy."

"I'm not busy. Not today, at least."

She couldn't be ungracious. And it would be ungracious to turn him away. "Okay, but don't think I've forgotten about your dad's basement. When do you want to drive over there? We'll have to assess what we're dealing with."

"Oh, uh, I haven't thought about it. Been getting settled. I'll just meet you over there sometime."

"Let me know when, and I'll get someone to watch the girls."

"You don't have to—"

"You didn't have to take over my projects or set up my Christmas tree, either." She straightened her shoulders. "I want to help. I'm going to help."

He didn't meet her eyes, but he nodded.

It hit her then. Even if she allowed herself to dream of getting remarried—which she couldn't—Dean, or any guy really, might not be interested in her. A single mom with twin toddlers was a lot to take on.

"Are the decorations out in the garage, too?" he asked.

"No, they're in the laundry room."

"We passed it on the way to your bathroom, right?"

She nodded.

"I'll go get them."

"Okay, I'll fluff these branches while you do."

They'd decorate her tree. Maybe even decorate a tree at his house later. Then she'd help him with the basement and be thankful when her house was finished. After that, her time with Dean would end.

She'd be left with good memories, a functional house and her girls.

It would have to be enough.

Chapter Five

If one more thing delayed him from getting started on Brooke's bathroom, he was going straight to the stables, loading Dusty in the trailer, driving out to Marc's ranch and checking cattle for the next three days. Dean had never fully grasped how stressful his dad's life as a builder could be. Almost nothing happened on time, and on the rare occasion it did, materials were missing or damaged, which delayed any progress he hoped to make.

The following Thursday morning, he parked in Brooke's driveway and took a minute to get his head on straight. All week he'd been trying to line up a crew to come out here. However, the time his dad had been in the hospital had put the subcontractors in a bind, and all but one had moved on to other projects. Patrick Howard's building needed that crew.

Looked like he was installing the cement board and sheetrock himself. The only construction projects he refused to do were electrical and plumbing. Too much could go wrong. At least Terry Burman had offered to help him with Brooke's bathroom.

On Monday, Dean had inspected all of the boxes his father had ordered for Brooke's bathroom. The shower tray was damaged, one of the boxes of tile was the wrong color, and the vanity had a chip in one of the doors. Dean had called the vendors. The new shower tray arrived yesterday, but the replacement tile wouldn't be here until late next week. A new vanity door should be arriving in ten to twelve days.

Dean opened the truck door and stepped outside. A cold wind blew. He remembered the old *ten to twelve days* from his late teens when he'd worked for his dad. He doubted they'd see the new vanity door for at least three weeks—a headache he'd deal with later.

It would be worth the headache to make Brooke happy, though. Every time he thought about her dark blue eyes and her sweet girls, something twisted inside him. He wanted to give her some peace of mind.

Decorating her Christmas tree on Saturday had made him feel even more comfortable with her than before. They'd talked about Christmas traditions and how neither had celebrated much over the past couple of years. When she'd offered to help him put his tree up, he'd shaken his head and told her he'd take care of it another time, that he was driving to Casper to see his dad.

He *had* gone to Casper, but that wasn't his reason for declining.

He liked Brooke. Too much.

Before he unloaded the materials from his truck, he checked his cell phone. Dad had left three messages concerning various projects. The man had moved into the rehab center on Monday and was slowly improving. The doctors still didn't think he'd be home until after the new year, though. They also warned it could be weeks after that before he'd be able to return to work.

Could he really act as Dad's surrogate for the next month or two?

Yeah, he could. He'd expected to feel out of his league, but his afternoon check-ins with Brenda energized him. Most of the remaining work on the schedule was on track to get finished.

As he unloaded the back of the truck, Terry pulled up and parked in the street.

"Howdy, Boss. Cold enough for ya?" Terry had recently turned sixty-four. Dean knew this because the man proudly announced it every time they spoke. On the shorter side with a protruding belly, Terry had a deep, bellowing laugh that erupted often and for no apparent reason. He seemed eager to be working with Dean, so that was good.

"Yeah, I hear it's about to get frigid." Dean wrapped his tool belt around his waist.

"Bah, this ain't nothing." A toolbox swung from his hand. "Ice storm of '84 made the North Pole look like the Bahamas. Never saw anything like it in my sixty-four years."

"I hope we don't see anything like it this winter."

"I wouldn't count on it…" Terry kept up a steady stream of chatter as they made their way up the driveway and porch steps. Brooke must have done more Christmas decorating. The porch posts were wrapped in red ribbon, two wooden reindeer with plaid bows flanked the welcome mat, and a cheery Christmas wreath hung from the door. Dean knocked, and within seconds, Brooke opened it.

"Brr, it's cold out there. Come in." Wearing a navy sweater and jeans, she rubbed her forearms. "Hi, Terry."

"Howdy, Brooke." He grinned, making a production of craning his neck. "Where are those two munchkins?"

As if on cue, Megan and Alice raced to the door.

"Dee!" One of the girls pointed up to Dean. He couldn't tell them apart. They weren't dressed the same, but everything else about them was identical. His heart gave a small tug at the fact that they were trying to say his name.

"Hey there." He bent, and to his surprise, one of the girls

opened her arms for a hug. He obliged, and the other twin held her arms open. He hugged her, too.

"Alice and Megan, Mr. Dean and Mr. Terry are fixing Mommy's bathroom."

One of the twins turned to Terry, who pretended to find a coin behind her ear. She laughed and laughed.

The other twin stood in front of him and thrust a floppy puppy his way. Her big, twinkly eyes would melt iron. If she'd handed him a live porcupine, he would have taken it. "How's Booboo today?"

"Woof."

He pretended to pet it and handed it back to her. She hugged it tightly and swayed side to side.

"Do you need me to show you the way?" Brooke asked. Looking at her pretty face, he melted in a different way. Yes, he wanted her to show him the way. And he wouldn't mind if she stayed right by his side until the day was over. There was something about her that drew him to her.

"I think we can manage." He attempted a smile, but he was pretty sure his lips stuck to his teeth. "Come on, Terry, this way."

As they headed down the hall to her bedroom, the aromas of waffles, Christmas spices and the baby aisle at the grocery store mingled together. Music from the living room played children's songs. One of the twins let out a loud laugh, and the other joined her.

All of it was as foreign to him as a rocket ship to space. But it intrigued him just the same.

This bright, warm home with little children and their joyful sounds made him want to settle in and stay.

But he couldn't. He was here to finish a job—and that was it.

"Here we are." Dean entered Brooke's bathroom. Terry

nodded as he stood next to him. "We're going to need to cut the cement board for the shower and the Sheetrock for the walls."

"Want me to set up the saw in the driveway?" Terry asked.

"That would be great. I'll measure everything. Oh, those two-by-fours in my truck? They're for blocking. We're adding a few grab bars in here."

"On it." Terry pivoted and left the room.

Dean took out the tape measure, a small notepad and a carpenter's pencil from his tool belt. He remembered the standard height to install a grab bar and handrail, but as he held the tape measure, he realized he needed the blueprint. He didn't know the heights to be accessible for people who used wheelchairs.

Striding down the hall, he tried not to catch a glimpse of Brooke or the girls. They made him long for things he didn't want to admit he'd purposely kept out of his life.

"Dean?" Brooke stood behind the long island and held a bag of cotton balls in one hand and a stack of paper plates in the other. Why? Who knew? He wasn't asking.

"Yes?" He gave the room quick once-over to see where the twins were—sitting at a child-size table.

"Why don't you have supper here, and we can head over to your dad's place later? Mom can watch the girls tonight. That way we can figure out what needs to be done in the basement."

He swallowed so hard his throat hurt.

"Uh..." Why couldn't he finish his sentence? The only thing she suggested that appealed to him was supper. That sounded right up his alley. The basement? Not so much.

She tilted her head and gave him a stern stare. "You said it needs to get done. Think about how happy your dad will be if he comes home to an organized basement. From what you told me, he's been wanting it done for a long time."

Dean stared at his feet. She spoke the truth. It *would* make his dad happy.

"It can be a Christmas gift for him." Her eyes had gone all sparkly again. "Supper is nothing fancy. Baked chicken and mashed potatoes."

Sounded good to him.

"We wouldn't have to actually go through any of the boxes tonight. We could just come up with a plan."

Maybe she was right.

"Okay. You talked me into it." He cleared his throat. "But we'll have to drive separately."

"Why?" She rounded the island, bending to place the paper plates on the table where the girls sat. Then she dumped cotton balls on the center of the table.

"Um, I may have to stay a while, and I know you've got to get back for the girls."

"Oh." She shrugged. "Okay. Do you think you'll be working here all day? Or do you have other jobs to go to? Supper will be ready around five."

"We'll be here for most of the day. We should be able to install the cement board and Sheetrock. We'll get a coat of mud on, too. It has to dry before we can sand it and put on another coat."

"Good. Oh, I forgot—feel free to use my garage. Marc warned me you'd need a spot with electricity. I can move my minivan into the driveway if you need me to."

"Thanks. I'll tell Terry."

She handed the girls glue sticks. "Are you ready to make snowmen?"

Dragging his gaze away, he forced himself down the short hallway to the front door.

Maybe the basement wouldn't be as bad as he thought. With Brooke there, the entire process might get finished in record time. At least she hadn't questioned him about driving separately.

A gust of wind blasted him as he stepped onto the porch. He shut the door behind him.

Do it for Dad. A Christmas gift, like Brooke said. Then the whole thing can be put behind you, and you won't have to feel guilty when you come to visit. It will be over. Done.

Visit? Where would he even be living next year? His future was murky. And he had a feeling it would be for a good, long while.

"Did you lose your key or something?" Brooke shivered next to Dean on the walkway leading to the steps of his father's house. The dark, overcast sky revealed zero stars, and the temperatures had been dropping all day. She wasn't sure why he was staring at the house with a strange look on his face, but she was too cold to wait around much longer. The sooner they got inside, the sooner she could get warm.

He shook his head as if he'd been lost in a memory. She understood that. She'd gotten lost in many memories in the weeks after Ross died. Maybe his dad's heart attack was still affecting him.

"Come on." She hurried up the steps and waved for him to join her.

His reluctance came through in each step, but he finally produced a key and unlocked the front door.

"See? That wasn't so hard." She playfully nudged him with her elbow and immediately regretted it. The man was all muscle…and stiff as a marble statue. Something about this house bothered him, but she didn't want to ask him about it. It had been difficult enough just getting him to join her tonight. That in itself had been a bit strange. Why had he insisted they drive separately?

She'd enjoyed catching up with him on Saturday while they'd decorated her tree. He was easy to talk to. His laid-back personality tempted her to share personal details with him that she tended to keep to herself.

Dean opened the door for her. Inside, she felt along the wall for a light switch. *Aha.* The overhead lights flashed on, revealing a comfortable—if dusty—living room with all the masculine details she would expect from a man like Ed. Hunting magazines on the end table, a huge television mounted to the wall and a pair of leather recliners near a big couch. Marc would feel right at home here.

"Should I slip off my shoes?" she asked.

"Don't bother. The basement's this way." He led her across the room to an archway where a large eat-in kitchen had a funky smell. Dean skirted the U-shaped counter, checked the sink and half grimaced, half gagged. "I should have come sooner. The dishes in here are full of mold."

"Fill the sink with hot soapy water. We'll let them soak while we go downstairs."

"Good plan." The faucet sputtered before letting out a steady stream of water. While Dean opened a lower cupboard to find the dish detergent, Brooke discreetly checked out the place.

"This is where you grew up, huh?"

"Yeah." He squirted dish soap into the sink.

"Is it weird coming back? When I moved to Texas with Ross after we were married, I never expected to live in my childhood home again. Marc had been living on the ranch by himself—Mom had bought a place in town by then—but he brought me back after Ross's funeral. I remember that day so vividly. Most of the days before and after are a blur. I stepped inside the living room where I'd grown up, and three things hit me at once. The first was an overwhelming feeling of love. I'd been loved in that house by my mom and brother. The second was the fact my dad still wasn't there. And that made no sense at all. He'd left us when I was twelve, and I hadn't seen him since. Why any part of me expected him to be there, I'll never understand."

She hesitated. She hadn't told any of that to anyone, not even Gracie, her best friend.

"What was the third?" Dean shut off the faucet and wiped his hands on a dish towel, then tossed it on the counter before joining her.

"The third?" She paused a moment. "I realized I didn't belong there. Not anymore. I wasn't a kid. I was a grown woman with two babies on the way."

"What did you do?" His brown eyes watched her intently.

"I went upstairs and cried all night. Silently. I cried and cried as quiet as could be."

"I'm sorry, Brooke." The way he said her name made her think he would have taken away every last teardrop if he'd had the chance.

"Thank you. I didn't realize it at the time, but moving back home was the best thing that could have happened to me. I needed Marc and my mom. And later, Reagan."

"When did you move into your house in town?"

"A little over a month ago."

"I wouldn't have guessed. It's homey, decorated. You settled in quickly."

"Yeah, I was excited to have my own place again." She gave him a smile. "The day Marc moved me to his ranch? I couldn't see a future. It wasn't even possible for me to dream I'd be where I am now."

"Is that good or bad?"

"Mostly good."

"I'm glad." He ran his hand through his hair. "I'm relieved that I don't have to stay here, even temporarily. Reagan's house has been working out great."

"Why does staying here—even temporarily—bother you?"

"I don't know." One shoulder lifted as he looked beyond her. "I guess, like you, I'm not a kid. I'm a grown man."

"And sometimes houses hold memories and old expectations that we'd rather forget."

He nodded. A moment passed between them: an understanding, a connection.

"Let me grab my notepad and pen." She turned away and fished both from her purse. "Should we see what's downstairs?"

"Yeah."

"Don't sound so excited." She grinned, but he didn't return it, just pointed to the doorway ahead and to her left.

He flipped on the light switch. The carpeted stairs ended at a landing area, then turned and continued for three more steps. Dean reached the bottom and turned on the main lights. A large, open room yawned before them, and Brooke took it all in. It was full of stuff.

"This is bad." Dean surveyed the space with his legs wide and hands on his hips. From her perspective, he looked like a warrior facing the enemy.

Maybe he was.

She tentatively joined him. Boxes, plastic totes and bins, bulging garbage bags and old furniture filled the space.

"Now I understand why you hesitated to come here. This is…" She didn't want to hurt his feelings or sound judgmental about Ed. It wasn't as if she didn't have several boxes in her garage she might never unpack. Who didn't have closets and attics full of things they needed to go through?

"Too much." He turned to her. "Too much to ask of you. I appreciate that you offered, but I don't expect you to—"

"It's fine," she said quickly. "We'll tackle it together. It looks worse than it is."

His face contorted as he stared at her. "I think you meant it couldn't get worse. There's so much crammed down here."

"And that's why organizing it will help your dad." She reassessed her initial reaction. Now that she'd had a moment to process it, she could see it more clearly. At least everything was contained in bins and bags and boxes. "How will we know what to get rid of, though? I'm sure some of this is special to him."

"There's a back storage area with shelves. He moved all of the important stuff there." He exhaled loudly as his stance softened. "All of this—" he extended his arms "—he wasn't sure what to do with."

"Then we can take care of everything in here without worrying if he'll miss it." She made sure to keep her tone upbeat. Dean was clearly overwhelmed and upset, and she wanted to make this as easy as possible on him. She took out her notepad and pen, then narrowed her eyes. "What do you think is in the garbage bags?"

"I don't know, and I don't want to find out."

"Mind if I take a peek?" She pointed her pen to the garbage bags on an old forest-green plush couch.

"Go for it."

The first garbage bag she came across had been tied with a knot, so she wiggled it loose and peered inside. "Old clothes. Men's. Probably your dad's."

"That's all?" He came over and looked inside.

"I'm not sure." Brooke pulled out old sweaters and jeans. "These are in good shape. The church's rummage sale would take them. Some of the church members store items through-out the year."

"Do you think Dad would be embarrassed to see other people around town wearing his old clothes?" Dean started untying the garbage bag next to hers.

"I'm not sure. Maybe. I guess you could ask him. Or Casper has several thrift shops where you could donate the clothes."

"That would probably be better. I'd ask, but I don't want him worrying about anything other than his recovery at the moment."

"Plus, it would ruin the surprise."

"Exactly." He wrestled the bag open. "This one has two old winter coats."

"See? This is already easier than you thought it would be."

He straightened and assessed the room. "Easier? Look around."

She chuckled. "We'll take it one bag, one box and one bin at a time. But first, let's get a general idea of what all is down here."

They opened the bins and unmarked boxes, and gathered odd items together. All the while, Brooke jotted notes. When they finished, they went upstairs. Dean zoomed straight to the sink and began scrubbing the dishes.

"Do you think we'll need a dumpster?" Brooke sat on a stool at the counter and tapped the end of the pen against the notepad as she reviewed her notes. "I wonder if anything down there is an antique? If it is, it should be sold."

"If we come across anything we aren't sure about, we'll put it along the wall and let Dad figure out what he wants to do when he comes home."

"Good plan. I like it." She jotted a list of supplies to bring next time—packing tape, more trash bags, sticky notes and permanent markers. "What about the boxes with the name Nancy?"

Brooke assumed they were his grandmother's. Her mom still had a few boxes of things that belonged to Grandma Dorothy. Mom had a hard time letting go, as did many people. Getting rid of Grandma's belongings was too painful, so they had stayed in the attic, unused for years.

"Nancy is my mom." Dean glanced up from where his forearms were buried in soap bubbles. "We can toss those boxes."

"After we go through them." Brooke wasn't tossing anything until she knew what was in it.

"She hasn't been back since I was a kid. She won't miss any of it."

"Still…" She didn't want to argue, but in this case, she needed to. "There might be other things in there, like important documents. Stuff gets stored in wrong boxes all the time."

His jaw clenched as he rinsed the final dish. Brooke tucked the notepad and pen back into her purse. From his body language, she'd guess he didn't agree with her, but he didn't want to argue about it, either.

"What day do you want to come back and dive into it all?" she asked.

"I don't know." He set the plate in a dish rack, wiped down the counters, hung the dishcloth over the sink divider and joined her. She stood, slinging her purse strap over her shoulder.

"The Christmas festival is Saturday, or I'd say we could start then," she said. "I suppose we could come over afterward."

"Christmas festival? Where's it at?" He nodded for her to head to the front door.

"Erica and Dalton Cambridge have been hosting it at the

Winston for the past couple of years," she said on her way to the entry. "This year they're having a Living Nativity with real animals."

"I suppose you're going with your mom."

"No, she's working at the bakery to give her employees the day off."

"Reagan and Marc?" He turned out all the lights, except for the one above them, and reached for the front door handle.

"Reagan's busy with Christmas orders at R. Mayer Chocolates, and Marc's working around the ranch."

Dean paused and looked into her eyes. Her pulse quickened. This brooding, gorgeous man should be off-limits. But when he looked at her like that...

"Why don't I meet you at the Christmas festival?" he said.

"Really?" Her stomach twirled at the thought.

"Yeah. You'll have your hands full with the girls. I can help."

"You're offering to help me with Megan and Alice? At the Christmas festival?" She didn't mean to sound so incredulous.

"Sure." He shrugged. "Why not?"

Why not, indeed? "Okay, meet me there at ten."

"I will. Oh, Terry's sanding the first coat of mud at your place tomorrow afternoon. I won't be there—I'm meeting Henry Zane at Dan Bagley's pole barn tomorrow for the inspection. Then I'm driving to Casper to spend time with Dad."

"Your father will love that." Her spirits dipped at the knowledge that he wouldn't be around, though. She liked spending time with him. "And I hope Dan's barn passes inspection."

"Me, too." He opened the door. "Let's get out of here. It's been a long day."

She ducked her chin into her scarf and shuffled down

the steps to the driveway. Dean held open the driver's door of her minivan.

"See you Saturday." He bent and hitched his chin to her. "Be careful driving home."

After he closed her door, she let the vehicle warm up for a minute. The girls were going to love exploring the festival with Dean. She would, too.

She'd better not read more into it, though. Her future had a big question mark around it, and Dean deserved more out of life than what she could offer.

Maybe he was just being nice.

The thought should have brought relief, but it merely dampened her good mood. *Enough of that.* A boyfriend wasn't on her Christmas list. Not even a steady guy like Dean.

Chapter Six

The day felt full of promise.

Out in the cold, crisp air, Brooke pushed the double stroller across the parking lot to the large event center on Winston Ranch. Already, people waited in line near the outdoor tents, where a petting zoo and Living Nativity were located. She could just make out a few reindeer in a portable corral beyond the tents. Decorated pines, garlands galore and an empty sleigh in front of Christmas trees gave the exterior of the Winston a hefty dose of yuletide cheer. This was the first holiday season since Ross died that she had even a twinge of Christmas spirit.

She hoped her leg didn't act up today. Earlier, her calf had felt twitchy, which didn't bode well. She probably should have stayed home, but this was one Christmas memory in the making she refused to miss. The girls were going to love it.

"Out, Mama!" Alice banged her little fists on the stroller bar.

"Out." Megan had clearly gotten the memo from her sister.

Brooke ignored them. The girls had been cheery all morning. She'd savored a full cup of hot coffee while they ate breakfast. Then she'd dressed them in matching outfits—something she typically didn't do—knowing the Christmas festival was sure to be packed, and it would be easier to keep track of them if they matched.

She glanced around the parking lot. Had Dean already arrived? She didn't see him or his truck. Best to wait for him in the event center. She forged ahead.

A teenager from church opened the door for her, but she still struggled to push the stroller inside.

"Let me help with that." Clem Buckley grabbed the front stroller bar and lifted it over the threshold. "Got your hands full, huh?"

"I sure do. Thanks." She usually avoided Clem. He always said exactly what was on his mind, and his words tended to cut like a saber through butter.

"How do you tell them apart?" he asked gruffly.

"Normally, I dress them in different colors. Megan is on the left, and Alice is on the right." She tried to keep her voice pleasant.

"Howdy there, ladies." His face softened as he wiggled his fingers in greeting to the girls.

Was Clem smiling? She couldn't recall a time she'd seen him smile. The girls weren't crying, so he must not be frightening them.

"You tell your mama to take you over to the kids' area. Get you some cookies and cocoa."

There was a human heart beating in Clem after all. She opened her mouth to continue the conversation, but he straightened, gave her a stern side-eye and hitched his thumb toward the table behind him.

"I've got to watch the donation jar. We're collecting for Hildy Youngkin's roof to be repaired. The insurance lapsed after Fred died, and one strong windstorm will tear those paper-thin shingles right off." He retreated a few steps. A large jar half-filled with bills sat on the center of the red tablecloth. "A tip from me to you. Skip the Living Nativity. That entire area smells. The camel stink will curl your toes, and I'm not certain your little ones won't get fleas—or something worse—in there."

"I'll keep that in mind." Brooke dug around in her purse until she found her wallet. She dropped a twenty-dollar bill into the jar, thanked Clem and pushed the stroller off to the side to wait for Dean. The girls began to fuss, and she bent to see what the problem was.

They wanted out. Which was absolutely not happening.

A tap on her shoulder made her turn. To her surprise, it was Mackenzie Howard and Cade Moulten. They'd gotten engaged in the fall and were planning their wedding for January, much to Christy's delight. Whenever Christy stopped by, Brooke heard all the latest about their plans.

She loved weddings. Her own nuptials had been small and perfect. She'd been blessed.

"Hey, guys." Brooke hugged Mackenzie, then Cade. "Did you just get here?"

"No, we decided to go through the Living Nativity first." Mackenzie smiled. "It's amazing. The girls are going to love it."

"That's funny, because Clem told me it smelled bad and the girls would get fleas."

"Leave it to Clem." Cade shook his head and rolled his eyes. "Ignore him."

"The owner assured me the camel and the alpacas have been treated for fleas and mites." Mackenzie, the local vet, took animal health seriously. "The girls will be fine."

"Good to know." Brooke hadn't considered fleas to be a problem in any way, shape or form, so she wasn't worried. Two older ladies from church stopped in front of the twins and began oohing and aahing over them, which was good since it distracted the girls from wanting to get out of the stroller.

"Mom should be here any minute. She's bringing Tulip." Cade put his arm around Mackenzie's shoulders.

"I'll watch for her." Brooke grinned. "The girls are obsessed with that little dog."

"We are, too." They caught up for a few more minutes before Cade and Mackenzie waved and walked away.

"Sorry I'm late." Dean, out of breath, came up to her. "Got here as soon as I could."

"It's no problem." Her heart practically fluttered in her chest. How ridiculous! She should not be this excited to see him. She studied him more closely. His face was flushed. "Are you okay?"

"I'm fine. I took Dusty for an early-morning ride, and I lost track of time. Sorry."

"Is that all?" She arrived late for things too often for her own personal taste. One of the girls would spill something or need a diaper change, and her careful timeline would collapse. "No big deal." She reached out and squeezed his hand, then gripped the stroller. The church ladies had moved on, and the baked goods section beckoned. "Shall we?"

"Lead the way." He stayed by her side as they strolled around to the various booths. She bought decorated sugar cookies in the shapes of dogs and cats. Dean bought blueberry muffins and peanut butter blossoms. More than one person insisted on giving the girls treats, and Brooke had to store most of them in the white paper bag with the cookies she'd purchased. The twins were hyped up enough without buckets of sugar in their systems, and both would surely want hot cocoa later.

"What do you think?" she asked. "The outdoor attractions first? Then the children's area?"

"Works for me."

"Oh, and I want to get a picture of us in the sleigh." If it turned out well, she'd frame it. A happy memory with her girls.

"I'll take it for you."

"You will?"

"Want to take it now?"

"Good idea. Let's do it while the girls are fresh. I think I'll leave the stroller in here. It's hard to push over uneven ground." After making sure Megan and Alice had their winter coats zipped and their little stocking caps on their heads, she carried Alice, and he took Megan outside.

"Good, the line isn't too long for the sleigh." Dean pointed. Megan pointed, too, and he laughed. "You're going in there, kiddo."

Brooke happily chatted with people who stopped to greet them. When it was their turn, she gave Dean her phone and climbed into the sleigh, settling Alice on her lap. Dean handed her Megan.

"Everyone say, 'Booboo.'" He held up her phone.

Megan and Alice clapped and yelled, "Booboo!"

He took several pictures, then jogged over and handed her the phone before taking Alice from her lap. "What now?"

She kept Megan on her hip as she stepped down, but her leg muscle gave out, making her trip and fall into Dean. With one arm, he steadied her. "Whoa, there. You okay?"

"I'm fine." Heat blasted her cheeks. Stupid leg. "Just tripping over my own feet."

He didn't say a word, but his eyes shimmered with concern. He kept his hand on her elbow to guide her toward the tents. She had the strongest urge to hold his hand or hook her arm in his. To lay a claim on him that wasn't hers to make. This wasn't a date. They were two friends enjoying the Christmas festival together. That was it.

"Let's check out this Living Nativity and hope we don't get fleas," she said brightly.

"Huh?"

She told him about Clem's warning as they made their way to the tent. After a brief wait in line, they were ushered inside, where John and Shirley Jones, a couple from church, wore makeshift robes. "Welcome to Bethlehem. You're about to go on a journey—a Christmas journey—similar to the one Mary and Joseph took over two thousand years ago. You'll pay your taxes and see the sights and sounds of the market. You'll stop at the inn and the stables. And you'll see shepherds worshiping a baby—our Savior, Jesus Christ."

They took it seriously, Brooke would give them that. She glanced up at Dean. With a solemn expression, he tipped the front of his Stetson and replied, "Thank you."

They carried the twins through the next section of the tent. Roger Pearl, Jewel River's dentist, was dressed like a soldier. He stepped into their path. "Halt. What is your purpose here?"

Megan took one look at Roger and started bawling. Alice joined her. Their wails were accompanied with fat teardrops on their cheeks.

"Oh, no, I'm sorry." Roger took off his helmet. "See, girls? It's me. Rog."

Brooke glanced at Dean. "I think we'll try this next year when they're a little older."

"Smart thinking."

"I'm sorry, Brooke," Roger said. "I never thought I'd scare them." He fished around where his pockets should have been, but his costume didn't have any. "Oh, fish sticks. Next time I see you, I'll have stickers for them. You two girls can have all the stickers, okay?"

"It's fine, really." The wailing continued. "We'll pet the reindeer instead."

"There's a shortcut through the back." He pointed behind him.

"Thanks."

They hurried out, and the girls quieted almost immediately. Megan's bottom lip still wobbled, but Brooke could tell the worst was over.

Brooke kissed Megan's cheek. "How about we go see the reindeer?"

Dean was rubbing Alice's back as her arms wrapped around his neck tightly. He whispered, "Shh. It's okay. I've got you."

Seeing him holding Alice, hearing him comfort her, made her stomach drop. Maybe enjoying the Christmas festival with him was a mistake.

Stop reading too much into it.

A couple of hours together wouldn't hurt a thing.

"Well, if it isn't Dean McCaffrey." A female voice carried. "I figured I'd see you around eventually."

Ten minutes after the Living Nativity fiasco, Dean turned his attention to Donna Marquez, one of his high school friends, waving to him from outside the pen.

He kept a firm grip on Alice's and Megan's hands in the reindeer pen. Brooke had been taking pictures, but had gotten waylaid by a little boy who wanted to talk to her.

"Hey, Donna," he said, slowly steering the girls her way. "It's been a while."

"Too long. How'd you get your hands on these babies?" Donna grinned and waved her hot pink gloves beyond him. "Hey, Brooke."

"Hi, Donna." Brooke grinned before turning her attention back to the little boy.

"How's your dad?" With dark curls tumbling from the

hood of her coat, Donna rested her forearms on top of the fencing.

He glanced down at the twins. They were getting antsy. He swooped Alice up on his right hip and Megan on his left. "He's improving. Ornery, though."

She let out a guffaw. "Ornery is only the start of it, I'm sure. Ed lives, eats and breathes construction. It can't help his blood pressure being out of the loop for this long."

"I'm doing everything I can to keep his blood pressure as low as possible." He smiled, firming his hold on Alice as she twisted her neck to watch the reindeer behind them.

"You're doing a great job. Henry said Dan's pole barn passed inspection, and Patrick Howard's relieved his service dog training center will be able to open on time."

"Thanks, but I didn't do anything special."

"I disagree." She narrowed her eyes and made a tut-tut sound. "Since when did you become so modest?"

"What about you?" Time to change the subject. "What have you been up to?"

"Got promoted to sergeant in the spring, and I met Andy in September." She glanced back and pointed to a tall man in a winter coat standing a few feet behind her. The man didn't smile, didn't move. He did nod, though. "Hey, Andy, this is my buddy from high school, Dean. The one I told you about. His daddy had the heart attack."

"Sorry about that. Having fun, Donna?" Brooke joined them. "Hey, Andy."

The man gave her a nod.

"We're having a great time," Donna said. "Not as much fun as you two seem to be having, though."

Dean stiffened. Did Donna think he and Brooke were dating? That they were a couple?

"You're having fun today, aren't you, Meggie?" Donna asked. "You too, Alice."

The twins. Right.

"Except for the Living Nativity. Too intense for them at this age." Brooke reached for Megan, and Dean handed her over.

"Uh-oh. Did Roger scare them?"

Brooke chuckled. "Yeah. He felt terrible."

"Well, I won't keep you. Bye, girls." Donna blew them kisses, and they blew kisses right back to her. "Bye, Dean."

"See you later, Donna."

Donna and Andy continued on their way, and Brooke began walking toward the corral gate. "Are you up for the children's area? It's inside."

"I'm up for it." He unlatched it and waited for her to exit before following her out of the reindeer pen.

"Have you decorated your tree yet?" She asked about his tree every time he saw her. And the answer was always the same. No.

But he didn't want to admit he had no plans to decorate one. "Not yet."

"Dean! You need to decorate it. Just think how nice it will be to come home to those twinkling lights."

"Mmm-hmm."

"Do I need to come over tomorrow and make sure it happens?"

"No, no." He shook his head. "I'll take care of it."

"Uh-huh." She didn't sound convinced. Inside the Winston, they unzipped their coats, found the stroller along the wall and laid the coats on top of it. Then they went to the restrooms to wash their hands.

When they returned, Brooke turned to him with wide eyes. "Oh, I almost forgot. Joey's movie. Let's go find it."

Brooke looked around and pointed to the left. "It looks like the kids' area is over there. Oh, look, a hot cocoa stand."

In no time at all, Brooke situated Megan and Alice on the large rug where several kids lounged in front of a big-screen television that played a movie.

"Why don't I get us some hot chocolate?" Dean whispered, bending over so only she could hear him and not the girls.

"Would you? That sounds good." Her grateful smile sent a pool of warmth down to his stomach. What was it about her? Was it this festival? It made him feel all ooey-gooey inside, and he'd never considered himself a softie.

"Be right back." First he checked out the movie. Instrumental Christmas music played, and a cat wearing an elf's hat walked past a fireplace. The twins pointed, their mouths rounding in Os as they yelled, "Kiki!"

Then a dog with antlers walked past the fire. One of the girls pretended to bark. Probably Megan. A bunny with a red cape hopped by the fire. The twins scrambled to their feet. "Bunbun! Mama, see?"

"I see. A Christmas kitty, doggy and bunny. Don't they look cute?"

Dean tore his gaze away from Brooke and the girls. The camera panned to a window with snow falling against a night sky. Then the three animals lay side by side on a rug in front of the fireplace. The words Merry Christmas danced on the bottom of the screen for several moments, and then the movie replayed. He noted both twins staring in rapt attention at the television.

A dozen people waited in line ahead of him at the hot chocolate booth, and he took the time to study the place. It seemed the entire town had turned out for the Christmas activities and bake sale.

This morning, as he'd ridden Dusty around the trails at the stables, he'd had second thoughts about coming. But there was something special about experiencing the event with the twins and Brooke.

The line inched forward, and he bought four cocoas with whipped cream topped with lids. He brought them in a drink carrier to the children's area. Brooke had settled the girls at a child-size picnic table, where they were coloring on printed sheets of snowmen.

"Here you go." He handed Brooke one of the cocoas.

"Thank you. I saved you a chair." She gestured to the folding chair next to hers.

"Should I give them these?"

"Not yet. Let's give them time to cool down. Besides, they're busy at the moment."

He sat beside her, enjoying how the twins clutched the crayons in their chubby fingers.

"We need to set a time to work on your dad's basement."

"What do you mean? We went there a few nights ago."

She laughed as if he'd said something funny. "All we did was figure out a game plan. We actually need to go through all the stuff."

"Do we?" Although his tone was joking, inside, he was dead serious.

"How about Wednesday night? My mom should be free to watch the girls."

Wednesday? So soon? He wanted to let out a loud sigh but took a sip of cocoa instead. "Uh, sure."

Brooke winced, set her cup on the floor and massaged her left calf.

"Everything all right?"

"Yeah." She let go of her leg and straightened. Her forehead creased as she picked up her cup. "My leg acts up some-times."

"What do you mean?"

"It gets weak. Cramps and twitches."

"Anything I can do to help?"

She shook her head, but the tightness in her face concerned him.

"How often does this happen? What do the doctors say?"

"Not that often." She shrugged. "They tell me to take it easy. I will when I get home."

"It's good that we're taking a break." He took another drink of the cocoa. Sweet. Warm. He hadn't had one in years, but could easily make it a habit.

Megan and Alice lost interest in their coloring sheets. They toddled over to Brooke and put their hands on her leg as they bounced. "Cocoa?"

"Yes, Mr. Dean got you some cocoa, too. What do we say?"

"Tank you!" Megan shuffled over to him and held up her arms.

"You're welcome." He picked her up and gave her a hug. The layer of toughness he'd forced on himself a decade ago melted away. He was beginning to understand why parents would do anything to protect their kids. These girls were precious.

"Me, me!" Alice held up her arms.

He laughed and set Megan back on her feet. Then he hugged Alice.

Brooke pointed to the table. "Once you sit down, I'll give you the cocoa."

They sat across from each other and beamed at her as she put the cups in front of them.

Alice took a sip and grinned. Megan followed. They only

spilled a few dribbles. Brooke wiped them with napkins, then winced.

"Here, why don't you sit again?" He wanted to take her hand in his. Reassure her he'd take care of whatever she needed. But they didn't have that kind of relationship.

Which left him wondering, what kind of relationship did they have?

"Thanks." Her face had paled, and fear filled her gaze. "I was going to return home soon, before the girls get crabby, but I think I'd better stay here for a while."

Any other guy would leap at the chance to drive her and the twins home. He wanted to be that guy.

He couldn't offer to drive her home, though. Couldn't offer much at all.

No, that wasn't true. He could do something. It might not be much, but it was better than nothing. "I'll stay with you."

The way her eyes lit up would have made someone think he'd offered her the moon. Did she expect so little out of life that him offering to stay with her made her grateful?

"Thanks, Dean. I appreciate it."

"It's no problem." He finished his hot chocolate and pushed the empty cup to the side. "Your husband would have loved this, huh?"

"Ross?" She frowned, blinking. The twins were licking the lids of their cups. "Yeah. He'd have loved it. He would have been protective of the girls. That was his nature. And he would have spoiled them, I'm sure. It's hard sometimes, thinking of what should have been."

What should have been. She *should* have been here with her husband.

And Dean should have been alone in Texas, checking cattle. Not enjoying himself here with her.

"I wish your husband could be here. I'm sorry you're stuck with me today."

"Never be sorry. I'm not stuck with you—I'm glad we did this. It's been really nice. Thank you."

Really nice.

For him, too.

They were quite the pair. Brooke had physical issues. He had emotional ones. And she needed someone she could depend on, not a guy like him who couldn't even drive her and the twins home when her leg cramped up.

He wasn't meant for Christmas festivals and families and a beautiful woman like Brooke. He'd simply finish her projects, deal with Dad's basement and move on.

She'd been pushing herself beyond her limits. And she'd let her enthusiasm about walking around the festival with Dean bulldoze the signs that she needed to slow down. It had only been an hour since she'd left the Christmas festival, but she probably should have driven home immediately after tripping as she got off the sleigh.

The signs that she needed rest had been there, and she'd chosen to ignore them. Being off-balance, fatigued, having the muscle weakness—not good.

Brooke leaned her head against the pillow she'd brought from her bed to the couch. She stared at the ceiling with her hands on her stomach. The girls were napping in their room, and she'd put a soothing Christmas playlist on the speaker. The mug of hot tea on the end table behind her was too hot to drink.

Dr. South's advice whistled through her brain. *Be mindful of your body. Keep your stress levels low. Don't overdo it.*

She constantly referred to her list of stress relievers she kept in her phone. *Lie on the couch, listen to soft music, sip hot tea, take a long bath, read a novel, watch a movie, do gentle stretches.*

All well and good if she wasn't raising active toddlers by herself. Was she being too optimistic thinking she could raise the twins on her own?

Closing her eyes, she tried to picture Ross. His sharp jaw and amused expression still stayed in her mind. She remembered how she'd clung to him right before he left on assignment. How he'd kissed her and held her as if he'd never wanted to let her go.

But he had let her go.

Neither of them had had any idea it would be their final moment together.

The familiar sadness seeped through her body, but it didn't feel as raw anymore. She supposed she was moving on…to what, though?

Dean's brown eyes, broad shoulders and gentle way with her girls kept opening her eyes to a potential future she'd never considered.

Her ankle and calf twitched as if to remind her she'd be a fool to consider dating again. Her health problems were real, and they were too much to burden Dean with.

God, forgive me for wanting things I can't have. Remind me You're enough. You'll always be enough for me and my girls.

Her eyelids drooped. Maybe she needed a nap as much as the twins did. Monday morning, she'd call the specialist about her leg. If the weakness was signaling her body was in danger, she needed medical advice.

Once again, she wished the bathroom were finished. If she had to use a wheelchair, the bathroom and ramp would be vital for her to live here with the girls. Anxiety spun around inside her.

Dean would complete everything. She could count on him to see her projects through. They'd finish his dad's basement—providing she didn't have a medical emergency anytime soon—and then they'd go their separate ways. She'd keep her romantic feelings to herself. It wouldn't do to burden him with her house *and* her heart.

She wasn't the kind of girl who could offer marriage and more children, and he might not be the type of guy who wanted either from her.

They were best off staying just friends.

But her heart was stretching past the friendship boundary already, and she couldn't seem to stop it.

Chapter Seven

"It's too cold to dig the holes for the new posts." On Wednesday afternoon, Terry's breath came out in visible puffs as he eyed the pile of old decking they'd finished tearing from the back porch of Brooke's house. "Ground's frozen."

Dean pushed and pulled on one of the old posts, trying to wiggle it loose. "These have to go. Did you call 811 yesterday?"

"No. I saw the forecast and figured I'd better talk to you before having the utility lines flagged."

Dean clenched his jaw. He'd specifically told him to call the number yesterday. He hadn't asked him to check the forecast. While Terry had been a big help so far, the man didn't always follow through with directions.

"We need to get these posts out and the new ones in. Soon."

"If you ask me, it should have been done in the fall." Terry pulled back his shoulders. "I've lived in Wyoming for sixty-four years…"

Here we go. If Dean had to hear one more mention of Terry's sixty-four years, he was going to march to his truck and drive to the stables to ride Dusty. He couldn't take it.

"I'm sure you're right, but this ramp needs to be installed before Christmas." He looked around the yard, trying to come up with a plan. He couldn't build the ramp until the old posts were removed. He also couldn't build the ramp until the new posts were installed. And Terry was right. The ground was frozen and probably would be through May.

Getting the old posts out wouldn't be a problem. McCaffrey Construction had machines for that. But he didn't want to tear up Brooke's yard by digging the new holes with a backhoe.

At least the bathroom was moving along. He and Terry had installed the shower tray on Monday. And yesterday, Dean had painted the walls. He'd tried to find a subcontractor to lay the tiles, but they were booked through mid-January.

He might not be an expert, but he knew the basics on how to set the shower and floor tiles. The replacement tiles had arrived yesterday. In the meantime, he wanted to get started on the ramp.

Which meant they needed to dig postholes, bringing him back to square one.

Think. This was Wyoming. Winter lasted forever. Nothing new there. Ranchers had to fix fences all the time, and that included putting new posts in the ground.

Dean pulled his phone from his coat pocket, tore off one glove and found Marc's number. He answered after one ring. "What's up?"

"Any suggestions on how to dig a posthole when the ground is frozen?"

"Are you kidding? I dig them all the time in the winter. Here's what you're going to do. Figure out where you want the holes and clear the area of anything flammable. You're going to cover those spots with metal ovens—don't worry, I've got a bunch of old metal protein supplement tubs on hand for that reason. We'll make some fires and cover them with the metal ovens. Let them burn a few hours, and you'll be able to dig those holes with no problem."

"What about embers and sparks?" Dean saw the potential in Marc's idea, but this was a residential area, and he had to keep in mind all of the nearby houses.

"I weigh down a small mesh screen over each smoke hole. Keeps the embers in."

They chatted a few more minutes and ended the call. Dean then explained the process to Terry, who brightened at the mention of fires and metal ovens.

"If we get us some marshmallows, we can make s'mores."

Dean blinked twice. Had Terry really just said that? "No marshmallows. This isn't camping."

"I didn't say it was. I just like a toasted marshmallow now and then. My mouth's watering just thinking about those burnt, crunchy edges."

Dean ignored him and dialed 811. After telling the operator Brooke's address, he pocketed the phone.

"Let's move the old deck boards to the back of my truck."

"What about these?" Terry pointed to the posts sticking out of the ground.

"We'll bring the digger over."

A grin spread across Terry's face. "Now you're talking."

Two hours later, the cement-encased posts had been removed, and all of the old materials were loaded into the back of Dean's truck. Terry waved goodbye, and Dean knocked on the front door to let Brooke know they were leaving.

"Come in." She smiled, waving him inside.

"Dee!" Megan and Alice barreled to him with their arms open wide.

He laughed and gave them both hugs. They each took him by the hand and attempted to drag him to the kitchen.

"Whoa, I can't go in there." He used his kid-friendly voice. "My boots are all muddy."

Their faces fell, and Brooke caressed the tops of their heads. "Go play for a minute while I talk to Mr. Dean."

"No, Mama." They both shook their heads. "No."

"Girls," she warned.

"Dee, Dee!" Alice clung to his hand.

"Alice!" Brooke sounded mortified. "Mr. Dean is working. He can't come in right now."

She stomped her little foot. Even when mad, the kid was cute. Dean held back a laugh. Megan whispered something in Alice's ear, and together, they ran off.

"Those two get more stubborn every day." She gave him her full attention. "What's going on?"

"The back porch is gone, so I put up a rail blocking the doorway to keep you or the girls from accidentally falling. I'm heading over to Marc's to pick up a few supplies, and I'll be right back."

"Maybe the girls and I could come with you. I wanted to pick up a novel from Reagan. She was supposed to drop it off today, but she forgot it at home."

Dean blanked. His palms grew clammy, and his chest grew tight.

Brooke could not come with him. Not if he was driving.

"Sorry," he choked out. "The truck's full." A lie, but a necessary one. "I can pick up the book for you if you'd like."

Was he imagining the question in her stare? Maybe.

"Of course." She shook her head in a self-chastising way. "You need your truck for supplies. I don't know why I thought we could all take my minivan. If you don't mind grabbing it for me, she said the book is on the kitchen counter And when you come back, we can head over to your dad's place."

His mind raced. What was she talking about?

"It's Wednesday. Basement. Remember?"

"Oh, right." He should have made an effort to sound thankful, but he was pretty sure he sounded like a man condemned. "I'll have to meet you over there."

As the words left his mouth, he wanted to take them back. Wanted to be a normal guy who could drive her wherever she wanted to go. He couldn't, though.

"Why don't we drive over together?" she asked.

"I can't."

"Why not?"

Because I get a panic attack every time someone gets in the passenger seat. I'm thrown right back to that night when I almost killed Lia. The wreckage... How did either of us survive?

"I just can't." The words came out with the speed and precision of a nail gun.

"But it would save on gas, and we live so close to each other."

"Brooke." He inhaled through his nose, feeling the nostrils flare. Was it anger? Or fear? If it was anger, he needed to bring it down right now.

"What?"

Hedging and lying were not the way to go. He'd simply tell her the truth and trust she'd understand. Even if he didn't understand it himself.

"I don't drive with anyone else in my truck—or any vehicle, for that matter."

"Really?" She blinked in surprise. "Why not?"

"I was in a bad accident—" No, he wouldn't sugarcoat it. "I take that back. I *caused* a bad accident. And I haven't been able to drive with anyone in the passenger seat since."

"How long ago?" She didn't look horrified. Yet.

"Ten years, give or take." He kept himself still and stood tall.

"What happened?"

He gave a slight shake of his head. "I don't want to talk about it."

"Were you hurt?"

"No." Only on the inside. The emotional scars refused to heal.

"Was anyone else hurt?" The words were gentle, and her eyes warm.

"No."

"But everything changed for you, didn't it?"

"Yes." How did she know? How had she put his replies together and come up with that?

"I see." No judgment. Just acceptance.

"You do?"

She nodded, a compassionate smile on her lips. "Life changes in an instant. There's before. There's after. And no matter how hard you try or how much you want to, you can't get back to before. You're stuck with after."

"Yeah." He wanted to say so much more. Wanted to thank her for putting into words what he couldn't himself. Wanted to tell her he'd get back to before—back to when he could drive with a passenger and not have a complete emotional breakdown. Back to when he had a social life and a job with a future.

Back to when he sort of liked himself.

But she was right. He was stuck with after. And he wasn't making promises he couldn't keep.

"I'll meet you at your dad's house at six-thirty." Her chin rose slightly. "We're going to make a dent in it. You'll see."

Dean searched her eyes for any trace of disgust, but all he found was her acceptance of what he'd told her. He didn't have the heart to tell her the last thing he wanted to do was go through those boxes in the basement. Not when something was probably down there—who knew where—that he didn't want to see, didn't want to remember.

He sighed. "Yes, I'll meet you there."

Snow blew diagonally across the road as Brooke neared Ed's driveway that evening. She didn't like driving in bad weather, but this was Wyoming. She'd never leave the house if she waited for clear skies. Tonight, however, it added a layer of stress she didn't need.

The leg twinges she'd experienced on Saturday had returned briefly Sunday evening. On Monday, she'd called the specialist to make an appointment. They couldn't get her in until January. When she'd called the clinic here in town, Dr. South referred her to the specialist and told her to get more rest. She'd expected it. She'd called the clinic many times about leg weakness and fatigue over the past eighteen months. They were probably sick of her.

If she was supposed to be resting, why had she insisted on working on the basement with Dean tonight?

She turned into the driveway and kept her gaze straight ahead until parking in front of the garage. Dean's truck wasn't there. Not surprising, since she was ten minutes early.

She probably should have stayed home and rested. The Christmas season had brought more activity than she was used to, and she'd been enjoying every minute of it. She'd finished wrapping all the homemade candles, and the gifts she'd ordered for the girls were beginning to arrive.

Just because she had energy, though, didn't mean she should deplete it. She'd have to take extra care not to overdo it tonight.

What Dean had told her earlier about his accident came to mind. Had he been drinking? Distracted? What had happened? And why had it affected him so deeply?

Headlights appeared in her rearview. He was here. Anticipation spread through her body.

As he parked, she got out of the minivan and retrieved her box of supplies. They braced themselves against the cold all the way to the front porch and didn't speak until they were both inside.

"What a night, huh?" Dean swiped off his coat and shook the snowflakes from his hair.

Brooke had a hard time looking away from him. She had the strongest urge to help him brush off those snowflakes. *Keep your hands to yourself.*

"What's that?" He pointed to the box she'd set on the floor.

"Tape, garbage bags, scissors, blank labels, markers." She eased out of her coat. Dean reached for it, and she smiled. He hung both their coats in the closet, and they headed to the basement.

"Oh, good. The kitchen doesn't smell anymore." She glanced over her shoulder on the way to the staircase.

"You're right." He grinned. "Scrubbing the dishes must have taken care of it."

When they reached the basement, Brooke moved to the side to catch her breath and rest a moment. Dean didn't seem to notice. He went straight to the couch where they'd found the clothes in garbage bags. Two more remained.

"I'll deal with these." He grabbed one of the bags and began untying it.

"I'll start looking through the boxes." In a minute or two. She needed to get her equilibrium first.

"Don't feel like you have to do anything," Dean said. "I'll take care of the heavy lifting."

Music to her ears. She missed having someone around to get things out of storage…and to kill spiders. She hated spiders.

Ross hadn't been around much for their marriage, though. He'd been deployed for most of it. She'd gotten boxes out of storage herself. Killed spiders herself.

Why did she long for something she'd never had?

Brooke looked at the boxes closest to her. Should she dive into them? Or work through the plastic bins?

Dean hauled two of the bulging garbage bags near the staircase, dropped them on the floor and resumed his spot at the couch.

She lifted the cover off one of the bins. A wireless phone, an answering machine, cords galore, and an empty box the phone had been packaged in greeted her. All of it looked hopelessly out of date. "I think we can safely donate this entire bin. Except for the empty boxes. I'm trashing those."

"What's in there?" He glanced up. She listed everything, and he nodded. "Donate, for sure."

"I have to ask—and I already know the answer—but have you decorated the tree at your house yet?" She didn't look up from the bin she was poking through. She wanted Dean to have the Christmas feels. Every night, she loved dimming the lights, wrapping up in a soft blanket and staring at her pretty Christmas tree after the girls went to bed.

"Not yet."

"I'll come over and help you. Just say when. I want you to walk into your house and experience that warm hug feeling you get from seeing the glow of the Christmas tree lights."

"Warm hug? From those prickly needles? If you say so."

"You know what I mean."

He smiled at her. "Yeah, I know."

They talked about their favorite Christmas memories for half an hour and moved things into piles. Trash. Donate. Sell. Keep. The things they weren't sure about, they packed together in the bins she'd emptied. Ed could decide what to do with them later.

Brooke reached for a box marked Office, but it was too heavy. "Do you mind lending some muscle over here?"

"Sure thing." His lopsided grin and shimmering eyes made her heart beat faster. It certainly wasn't the taxidermied prairie dog she'd come across in the previous box, although that had given her a scare. He carried the box over to the coffee table. "Now that the couch is cleared off, you can sit on it while you're sifting through Dad's treasures."

"I like that. Sifting through your dad's treasures." She opened one of the flaps. "If anyone went through the boxes in my attic, they wouldn't think they were treasures. They'd see a bunch of junk."

"That's mostly what I'm seeing here." He went to the other side of the couch and hauled a crate of vinyl records over. "Why do you keep yours?"

"I suppose it's not junk to me." She smiled at him. He was staring at her, and she wasn't sure why. She turned her attention to the contents of the box. "I think this one must have been marked wrong."

"Why do you say that?" He shuffled through several records.

"I spy someone's rodeo trophies," she singsonged. Then she faked an enthusiastic grin as she lifted one up.

"Nothing like gold-sprayed plastic to make you feel like you're a winner." He shoved the records back in the crate. "Vinyls are popular again. I'm putting these in the sell pile."

"Good plan." She set each trophy on the coffee table and worked through the rest of the box. An old computer mouse, too many random ink pens to count, a mug shaped like a moose head and a plastic grocery bag filled with Matchbox cars and candy wrappers. "I don't think these candy wrappers are worth anything, but the cars might be."

Dean strode over and peeked in the bag. "Seriously? Why didn't Dad throw this away?"

He took the bag from her and tied the handles into a knot.

"Little boys would love those cars." She held out her hand to take it back. "Church rummage sale?"

"Fine. I'm getting rid of the trash in here, though." He sighed and opened the bag again. Took out each car. Reached in and dug around.

Then his hand stopped. He pulled out something, stared at it with an odd expression and quickly shoved it in his pocket before wadding up the bag and taking it over to the trash pile. "We've gotten a lot done tonight. Why don't we call it quits? I'll follow you back to town. This weather could make the roads slick."

"You're probably right. I don't like driving when it's snowing and the wind picks up."

With a serious expression, he nodded. "This is going faster than I thought it would."

They both surveyed the large space. They'd cleared about a third of the floor already. Progress.

"When are you visiting your dad again?"

"Tomorrow."

"In that case, why don't we load your truck with the pile of donations? You can drop them off at the thrift shop in Casper." She took out her cell phone, searched for ones close to the rehab center and texted him the results. "There. You have at least three to choose from."

She hefted one of the garbage bags and started up the staircase.

"Wait, you don't need to carry anything. I don't want your leg to bother you again." He reached for the bag. His calloused palm grazed the back of her hand, launching her back to her teen years and the million crushes she'd indulged in. She liked this guy. A lot.

Why wouldn't her brain get the memo that she was a widow with twin daughters, not a single woman in her prime? *If you care about him, you won't even consider a future together. You could be paralyzed or die young. And he'd be stuck dealing with the aftermath. It wouldn't be fair to him. Stop being selfish.*

"I think I can handle this. It's light." She yanked the bag her way. "You can get the other stuff."

He met her gaze for a moment too long, then nodded. She continued up the stairs. When she reached the top, she wasn't sure if her heart was racing due to overexertion or from the lingering sensation of Dean's hand grazing hers.

Either way, it was good they were calling it a night. She couldn't fall for Dean McCaffrey. Not now. Not ever. Not with her uncertain future.

Chapter Eight

"**D**id you bring me crullers?" Dean's father finished tying his running shoes and rose to his full height on Friday afternoon. He wore dark gray sweatpants and a Wyoming Cowboys T-shirt. He looked like he'd dropped ten pounds in the short time he'd been in the rehab center. His face was still pale, though, and he took a moment to catch his breath.

"Crullers? No." Dean shook his head, pretending to be offended. "You're supposed to be eating healthy."

"Anne's crullers *are* healthy." He dropped into one of the chairs by the window. "They give me the will to live."

"I brought you the next best thing." He held up the paper bag with an Annie's Bakery sticker on the side. "Her low-sugar, high-protein applesauce muffins."

"Low sugar?" His dad pulled a face. "Are you punishing me, son?" He muttered something about tasting like cardboard, and Dean decided to ignore it.

For the first time since getting the call about the heart attack, Dean truly believed his dad would make a full recovery. Relief made him tighten his grip on the bag.

He'd spent yesterday morning at McCaffrey Construction's office in town going over unfinished business with Brenda. Then he'd headed to the various jobsites before hurrying to Brooke's house.

Sadly, building the ramp was on hold. The utility companies were dealing with severe weather in several counties, and they wouldn't be out to her place until next week to mark the lines.

Thankfully, between yesterday afternoon and this morning, Dean had been able to install the grab bars in her bathroom, and he'd laid the shower tiles. As long as the new vanity door arrived by the end of next week, her bathroom would be finished by Christmas.

He was certain of it.

What he wasn't certain of was how to deal with the locket he'd found in that bag of toy cars Brooke had handed him in the basement Wednesday night.

He'd known what it was the instant he'd spotted it. The one thing he'd hoped would stay lost forever.

Twenty-three years ago, he'd stolen the locket from his mother the week before she'd moved out permanently. He'd been eight.

Why had he done it? Why had he taken the necklace from her? He'd regretted it almost immediately. Over the years, he'd wondered what had happened to it. And now he knew.

When he'd gotten back home after making sure Brooke arrived to her house safely, he'd tossed the locket into the dresser drawer with his socks, where it had been burning a hole ever since.

He hadn't opened it to see the photos inside.

He knew what he'd find.

And he didn't want to see them.

"I might as well try one of those tough, nasty muffins." Dad motioned for him to hand him the bag. Dean brought it over. "If Anne made them, they might not be so bad."

His cheeks still had a hollowness to them. Dean could see why he needed to be here rather than home.

"Hard day, huh?" Dean pulled a chair over to sit across from him and leaned forward to rest his forearms on his knees.

"Yep." Boy, he looked tired. "They had me on the station-ary bike for thirty minutes."

"Are you sure they aren't working you too hard?" Should he find one of the nurse's aides and ask them about it?

"They're working me hard, but I need it. I feel stronger. I'm sleeping better, too. I didn't realize how out of shape I was—and how much the heart attack and surgery took out of me."

"Brooke said the same about her stroke." When Dean had finished at Brooke's place yesterday, he'd hung around talk-ing to her for a long time. She'd explained her daily routine while in the rehab center. It made him appreciate what she'd been through even more than he had before. The woman was a fighter. A good mom. A great listener.

A friend.

His friend.

"She would know. It does make me feel better." Dad took a large bite of the muffin and didn't continue until he'd chewed it. "What's going on with the business?"

He fought a twinge of disappointment. His father always wanted updates on the construction projects, but he never seemed to want updates about him personally. Not that he expected him to care when he was dealing with so much, but Dean had a lot on his mind beyond McCaffrey Construction.

He was confused. About his future. About his feelings for Brooke. About the fact he actually enjoyed being involved with his father's business and didn't miss ranching as much as he thought he would.

"Everything's on track." Dean filled him in on Brooke's bathroom, Patrick's building and a potential new construc-tion house Brenda had gotten a call about yesterday.

"Did you set up an initial meeting with them?" Dad fin-ished the muffin and wiped the crumbs from his hands.

"Not yet—"

"What's the holdup? We don't turn down business if we can help it."

"I didn't turn down business." Frustration built. This was how his temper always ignited—Dad made assumptions, Dean justified himself, and before he knew it, they'd be going round and round, tempers escalating. *You're older now. More mature. You don't have to react.* "I needed to talk to you before I set up the initial appointment."

His father frowned. "Me? Why?"

"To make sure you want to take the job. Do you think you'll be able to handle adding it to your busy schedule? The couple wants to break ground this spring."

"That gives us plenty of time." He had a far-off look in his eyes. "I'll be home around Christmas. Back to work the beginning of January. I've got a few basement remodels starting in February. Yes, the spring will be fine."

Dean had his doubts. "Have the doctors told you you'll be home at Christmas and ready to work in January?"

"Doctors?" He scoffed. "I've got it covered. I'm doing my part. Sitting through the nutrition classes and listening to them jabber on about stress management. Next week, they're getting me on the elliptical machine. I'm not looking forward to it, but it's what I've got to do to get out of here and have my life back."

Dean had been avoiding thinking about it, but when Dad got his life back, where did that leave him?

"And, son, I know this isn't something we talk about, but I'd sure like for you to join me at McCaffrey Construction. You're doing a good job. Clem Buckley and Christy Moulten visited me yesterday, and they said everyone around town is impressed with how you've stepped up."

"Clem and Christy came together?" He'd chew on the compliment later. First he had to deflect the topic of him joining the family business. Didn't need a case of heartburn on an otherwise fine Friday.

"Yeah." He let out a throaty chuckle. "He's giving her driving lessons, and from what I can tell, they aren't going all that well. Those two bicker like an old married couple."

"Huh."

"You don't have to give me an answer today. Just consider it. That's all I'm asking."

Younger Dean would have brushed him off with a curt reply. Older Dean didn't have it in him. "I'll think about it."

Dad blinked several times before giving him a firm nod. "All right, then. Now, how's your horse? Christy mentioned you're stabling Dusty at Cade's stables. We did a bang-up job on that project. I worried we wouldn't finish it before his deadline, but we stayed on track and got it done. I had to bring in subcontractors from Casper."

"Dusty's thriving. Trent takes care of him whenever I can't be there."

"You and Trent used to run around together, if I recall. Have you been catching up?"

"Yeah, I see him at the stables every morning. And I went over to Ty's place when I first got to town."

"That kid's a hermit." He made a tsking sound. "He needs to get out more. Hiding away on his ranch isn't doing him any favors."

"I don't know about that." Hadn't Dean done the same for the past ten years?

"I do. Ty's broken heart is still broken. Probably always will be. But that doesn't mean he can't have a life."

"He has a life."

"The one he's living is no life."

The urge to argue tugged at him, but he kept his mouth shut. What would it accomplish?

"Dean?" Something in Dad's tone made him glance up. "What?"

"Why are you staying in Reagan's old place?"

Oh. That.

"It's closer. Makes for a shorter drive here."

"Is that the only reason?" The vulnerability in his expression tweaked his conscience.

"No." Maybe they didn't need to tiptoe around touchy subjects anymore. Maybe they could move past them. "I wanted to be close to Dusty. Ty and I are more alike than you think."

"I know why Ty hides away. I don't know why you do."

Tiptoeing was one thing, but full transparency was another. Dad's stress levels were supposed to be kept to a minimum. Even if Dean wanted to tell him about the car crash and events leading up to it, this wasn't the time or the place.

"I'll tell you about it when you're out of here and back home."

"How bad was it?" Fear flashed in his eyes. "Whatever it was that caused you to hunker down on that ranch in Texas?"

"I'm here, aren't I?" He attempted to smile. "I'll tell you when you're home."

His father studied him for what felt like ten minutes before nodding. "I'm holding you to it. I want to know what shook you up so bad."

"Fair enough." Dean exhaled a resigned breath.

Eric, the nurse's aide, entered the room. "Are you ready for your stress management class, Ed?"

"I'm ready for a nap." His dad gave the bed a longing glance.

Eric chuckled. "Plenty of time for that later."

Dean rose and gave his dad a big hug. "I'll be back on Sunday after church."

"Okay. Oh, and Dean?"

"Yeah?"

"Bring some more of those muffins. They were pretty good."

He grinned. "Will do."

As Dean strode down the hall to the entrance, he smiled at an older woman pushing a walker. Then he nodded to a man in a wheelchair. His dad was blessed to be leaving this place in decent health. Not everyone had that luxury.

He pushed open the door and went out to the parking lot. It was windy and cold. He shoved his hands into his pockets and ducked his chin as he strode to his truck. He had the whole night ahead of him, and he knew exactly what to do with it.

He'd stop at home, change his clothes and drive out to Dad's place. It was time to get serious about finishing the basement. It was the least he could do for the man.

Why couldn't she stay away from him? Early Friday evening, Brooke held Megan's hand and had Alice on her hip as she knocked on Dean's door. She'd been on her way to her mom's when she saw his truck in the driveway of Reagan's old house. Instead of driving past, like any normal person would, she'd pulled in and parked. To get an update on his dad. At least, that was what she was telling herself.

The truth was more complicated.

He'd been opening up to her, and she'd been sharing more with him, too. She felt safe talking to him.

That alone should have prevented her from stopping by.

Maybe she should leave. Yes, she definitely should march back down those porch steps and pile the girls into the mini-van. But just as she began to turn away, the front door opened. Dean, clean-shaven and wearing jeans and a sweater with the sleeves pushed up his forearms, blinked, then grinned and held the door open for her to enter. "Come in—get out of the cold."

"Dee! Dee!" Alice twisted and held both arms out to him. Megan dropped Brooke's hand and held up her arms, too.

He laughed and took Alice from her. After settling her on his left hip, he reached down and hauled Megan onto his other one. The move was so quick and easy—the man could clearly handle two toddlers, no problem.

"What brings you here?" He turned and made his way to the couch up ahead, and she followed. The twins were trying to tell him something, but it sounded like gibberish to her ears. He gave Alice his full attention before switching to Megan. "A dog? You got to pet a dog?"

How he'd deciphered *dog* when they'd been speaking over each other, she had no clue. But it was true. She'd paid Christy Moulten a visit this afternoon, and the twins, as usual, had been enamored with little Tulip, her Pomeranian.

"Tutu go woof!" Alice opened her hands as her eyes grew round.

"Tutu soft." Megan had a shyer way about her.

"I've got to meet this Tutu, huh?" He set them on the couch and sat between them. They both nodded through sparkling eyes.

Brooke sat in an adjacent chair. "Sorry to barge in like this. We won't stay long. I wanted to see how your dad is doing."

"He's good. Today I can honestly say I think he'll make a full recovery. I can't put my finger on it, but he seems to have cleared a hurdle."

"That makes me so happy." She put her hand over her heart. She knew exactly what he meant. "I remember the moment I knew I'd be able to walk unassisted again. That day filled me with hope and purpose. It gave me the drive to keep going, even when it was hard."

"He's determined. Your mom's muffins were a hit, by the way."

"I'm not surprised. She has a special touch when it comes to baked goods. They're all amazing." The girls had climbed onto his lap and were squished together, holding hands.

Oh, my. What a picture they made. She really should have kept driving.

"He specifically ordered me to bring more of them when I visit him after church on Sunday."

"I'm on my way to Mom's now. I'll pass the message along to her." She gave the room a once-over. "Where is your Christmas tree? Don't tell me you still haven't put one up."

"I'll get around to it."

She didn't want to badger him about it anymore, but she'd say one more thing before letting it go. "I want you to have something heartwarming and joyful to see every night. You deserve to enjoy the Christmas season."

Something in his gaze brought a flush of heat to her cheeks. If she wasn't mistaken, it was attraction. She reveled in the fact he saw her—the real her, the mom, the widow, the survivor of a stroke—and he still liked what he saw.

After all her lectures to herself, triumphant was the last feeling she expected to have.

Alice held on to his sweatshirt as she pulled herself up to stand next to him. Megan, not wanting to be left out, did the same. And to Brooke's shock, the girls each planted a kiss on one of Dean's cheeks. His face grew red as he beamed at them. Then he held both of them tightly, and they leaned against his shoulders.

"Well, that was awfully nice," he said.

"Wuv, Dee." Alice nodded solemnly.

Megan nodded, too. "Dee, wuv."

Brooke's heart couldn't take it. Her girls were as into him as she was. And on that note, Brooke figured she'd better go. She stood and reached for Megan, who waved her away with a "no." Alice did, too.

Fantastic. The girls preferred him to her and were on the verge of a tantrum.

"Come on, ladies," she said. "Grandma's waiting for you to help decorate reindeer cookies."

"Gwammy!" the girls shouted.

Phew. Sticky situation averted.

Dean rose and carried the girls to the door, then set them down.

"What are you doing tonight?" she asked as she reached for the handle.

"I'm heading out to Dad's place. Figure I can work on more of those boxes."

"Want some help?"

"I couldn't ask you to do that. It's Friday night. And your mom's expecting you."

"Mom is expecting the girls. She won't mind." She watched his expression carefully. Something held him back from accepting her offer, and her earlier triumph deflated. The girls wandered back to the couch. Great. "Unless you want to be alone."

"That's not it. I guess I just feel bad." He shrugged. "Christmas is less than two weeks away? You should be watching movies and drinking eggnog, not digging through dusty old boxes in my dad's basement."

"Maybe I want to dig through dusty old boxes."

"No one wants to do that." His eyebrows drew together.

"It's not the boxes, Dean. It's the reason behind it."

"My dad."

"And you."

"Me?"

The surprise in his tone made her question how truthful she should be. Then she tossed off her reservations. She hadn't made it this far—losing her husband, raising twins on her own—to be too scared to say what was on her mind.

"Yes, you." But then reality stepped in. Her health. Her future. "We're friends. You're finishing my house. I'm helping you with Ed's basement. That was the deal we made."

The light in his eyes dimmed, and it hurt her to see it. She'd reduced their relationship to a bargain, when what she felt was far more than that.

"In that case, I guess I'll meet you over there." His tone was flat.

She'd hurt him. Why was this so hard? Why wasn't she being honest about her feelings?

Because she wasn't supposed to have these feelings.

She couldn't leave it like this, though. "Wait, that came out all wrong."

"I think it came out exactly as you intended."

"You're right. I deserve that." She stared down at her boots, then met his gaze once more. "Our friendship took me by surprise." She tried to find the right words. "And it's more than that. I feel close to you."

The shimmer in his eyes returned, and he took a step forward. "I feel the same."

"But I...well...there are things that prevent me from getting too close."

"Like twins?"

"No, not really." She wrung her hands together. "Like my risk of another stroke and what it means for my future."

"I thought that's why you've been remodeling your house."

"It is." She nodded, swallowing the fear stuck in her throat. "But it's more than that. I don't see marriage again in my future. And I definitely don't see more children."

"Why not?"

"My doctors warned me about the dangers. My stroke risk would be too high during a pregnancy and for the first three months postpartum. I'm not willing to chance it."

His mouth opened slightly then closed again. What was he thinking? Why wasn't he saying anything?

She could guess why. If he'd harbored any deeper feelings for her, she'd just squashed them.

"Come on, girls," she called. "We're leaving."

"Let me carry them to the van." He slipped his feet into slides, picked up Megan and Alice from the couch and followed her out onto the porch and down the steps. "I get it, you know."

She buckled Megan into her seat and looked over her shoulder. "You do?"

"Yeah." He handed her Alice, and she got her settled. Then she pressed the button for the sliding door to close. "I don't see marriage in my future, either."

"You? Why not?" She barely noticed the cold as she stood inches from him.

"My reason isn't noble like yours." He shrugged. "I can't marry someone if I can't even drive her to church on Sunday."

Oh. She'd forgotten about that. Tilting her head, she stared at his earnest face. "She might not mind driving *you* to church."

"I'd mind."

"Want to give it a try later?"

"What do you mean?"

"I'll drop off the girls and come back here. We'll see what happens."

"No." The color drained from his face. "No."

"One try." She held up a finger. "I'll hop in the passenger seat of your truck, and if it's too much, we'll drive our own vehicles to your dad's house."

"You don't know what you're asking."

"Okay." She held out her palms. "Forget it. I'll meet you there instead."

Reaching for the door handle, she paused as Dean gently touched her arm.

"Wait." The muscle in his cheek flexed. "I'll try. But it's not going to be pretty."

"I don't expect it to be." She opened the door, got inside and started the van. "I'll be back in ten."

He nodded. Then she backed out of his driveway with her heart racing.

She'd intended to set him straight about the limits of their friendship. Talk about backfiring. They might both be saying they didn't see marriage in their future, but did they believe it? Why did she spend time with him—even if coming back would help him get over his fear—if she wanted to keep their friendship out of the romance zone?

Too many questions she couldn't—wouldn't—answer.

For now, she had a Friday night wide-open with Dean Mc-Caffrey, and she was going to make the most of it.

Of all the stupid things to agree to, this one took first place. But he wouldn't get a plastic trophy for it.

Dean paced in his driveway as he waited for Brooke to return. He cupped his bare hands to his mouth in an attempt to warm them. His heart was beating way too fast.

He could *not* do this. He couldn't let Brooke see him shut down. Couldn't bear to witness her disgust at his incapability of doing the simplest of tasks.

Anyone with a license could drive with a passenger next to them. Anyone. Except him.

Maybe it's better this way. She'll see for herself. Then you can leave, and she'll never think of you as more than a friend again. Isn't that the goal? This will accelerate the process.

He paused. Closed his eyes for a moment.

What if he *was* willing to explore a deeper relationship with Brooke?

That would open up another bag of problems. Because she'd made it clear she wasn't doing forever with a ring on her finger again. And he wasn't a casual dating type of guy.

Her minivan pulled to a stop in front of the house. She parked and got out.

"Are you ready for this?" she asked as her dark hair blew in the breeze.

"No."

Her lips twitched into a soft smile. "I know."

Her kindness, her understanding—that was what made him straighten his shoulders and glance at the truck. He knew exactly what was going to happen when they got into it.

Maybe he was tired of hiding. Tired of pretending he was like any other guy out there.

He cracked his knuckles. "I've tried before."

She wasted no time getting into the passenger seat of his truck. He raised his face to the sky. *God, I can't do this.*

A Bible verse he'd memorized raced through his mind. *I can do all things through Christ which strengtheneth me.* He regularly read the book of Philippians from his old King James Bible, and chapter four, verse thirteen, was one of his favorites.

Okay, God, I'm counting on You.

He got in and sat in the driver's seat. Pushed the start button. Let the engine purr while he attempted to clear his mind. *Pretend she's not next to you.*

As he glanced her way, the gravity of the situation weighed on him. Brooke, with her shiny hair and trusting eyes, was sitting in his truck despite his warning.

The memory of the crash was like a jolt through him. The crunch of the metal, the hiss of the valves.

As he stared at the dashboard, his breathing grew shallow. So shallow he began to gasp. Sweat broke out across his forehead. Dizziness forced him to grip the wheel, and his hands, moist with sweat, slipped on it.

He couldn't put her in danger.

Without giving it another thought, he jabbed the start button to turn the truck off. Dropping his head into his hands, he stared at his lap, blinking, gasping, trying to find normal, but it was nowhere to be found.

Why couldn't he breathe? Was he going to die?

The foggy feeling grew worse. He dared not think about Brooke or how she was reacting to all this.

"Dean, I'm here." She slipped her arm around his shoulders and gently rubbed his biceps. "It's okay."

It's okay? Was she serious? He fought for breath as his heart pounded. Moments later, he knew he'd gotten through the worst of it. As his breathing slowly returned to normal, he became aware that tears had fallen down his cheeks, and he discreetly swiped them away before raising his head.

"It's not okay." He shot her a sideways glance. "Nothing about this is okay."

She softly rubbed his upper back. "We're still in the driveway. Nothing happened. We're safe. Come here." She shifted, holding her arms out. Feeling foolish, but needing her embrace, he let her wrap her arms around him.

Her hug was like walking into a warm room, fire roaring, during the coldest ice storm. Like being tucked into the softest bed after climbing a mountain. Like taking shelter in a bunker during a tornado.

Her embrace was the safest place on earth.

When she eased back, his hands were trembling. He stared

into her big eyes, so close to his, and his gaze dropped to her lips. She didn't back away. No, her hand cupped his cheek, leaving him shaken, but not from the panic attack.

Without another thought, he slid his hand around the back of her neck and let his fingers creep into her hair. So soft. Just like her.

He needed her. Wanted to kiss her.

They'd both said their pieces earlier. This relationship couldn't go anywhere. But his heart didn't care.

"Kiss me, Dean," she whispered.

He didn't need to be told twice.

As soon as his lips touched hers, all the pain and worry and shame fled from him. She was peppermint sticks and hope and all the things he'd lacked for so many years. She pressed closer to him, and her touch made him bold. He explored her mouth and savored the feel of her silky hair between his fingers. Then he ended the kiss.

What was he doing? He could not kiss Brooke in his driveway. Couldn't kiss her anywhere.

Neither of them wanted a relationship. They both had their reasons. He'd proven to her he wasn't husband material, even if she changed her mind. Flattening both palms on his thighs, he dared not look at her.

"Wow," she said softly, sitting back into her seat with her fingers touching her lips. "Why don't you start the truck again?"

"What? No." He'd kissed her, and that was her response? Hadn't she seen him fall apart? Shouldn't she be yelling at him for kissing her? Or shaking her head in pity that having someone in the passenger seat affected him like this?

"Just start it." Her tone wasn't angry or judgmental. She sounded understanding. "We'll sit here. We'll stay parked."

He rolled the idea over in his mind. If they didn't leave

his driveway, he couldn't crash the truck. They'd be safe. He couldn't see any harm in it, so he forced his finger to press the button again. The engine rumbled, and he let his head fall back against the headrest.

"How much of the basement do you think we'll be able to get through tonight?" she asked.

She wanted to discuss the basement? Now? Visions of the crash flirted around the edges of his mind, but he directed his thoughts to the boxes in the basement.

"I'm not sure. It depends on what we find."

"Are there any more trophies I should know about?" she teased.

"If there are, I don't know what they'd be for." His jaw would shatter if he didn't loosen it. "Sixth-grade archery, maybe."

"I won a trophy in fourth grade for the triple jump on track and field day. I only won it because everyone else scratched."

His mood lightened a fraction. "It's still a win."

"This was, too." Her deep blue eyes captured him. "We've been like this for almost a minute."

He dragged his gaze away and stared ahead at the garage door. "Yeah, well, a minute is nothing to be proud of."

She placed her hand on his forearm. "It *is* something to be proud of. This was excruciating for you, and I think you're brave for trying."

An incredulous laugh slipped out. "Brave? I don't think so."

"You are brave." She gave his arm a squeeze before sitting back again. "I'm going to drive over to your dad's house now." She opened the door.

"Wait." Confusion crept in. "You're leaving? Now?"

"Yeah." She stepped onto the driveway. "Why?"

"I thought you'd want me to—"

"No." Her tender smile tore at his emotions. "You don't

ever have to drive me anywhere, Dean. But if you want, I have the number of a counselor you can talk to. He helped me last year after the stroke. I wouldn't have been able to move out of Mom's place if I hadn't committed to several sessions with him. He helped me see things in a different light."

"What kinds of things?"

"My fears. He gave me strategies to handle my worry about having another stroke."

Dean didn't say anything. The fact she'd spent a huge chunk of money making her home accessible made him think the counselor hadn't done a very good job. Did Brooke really believe she'd become disabled anytime soon?

"The only way I could handle moving out and raising the girls on my own was knowing I had a backup plan. My biggest fear is losing my ability to raise the twins. So I'm taking measures to retain that ability. Everyone around here thinks I'm overreacting, but they haven't been in my shoes."

Put like that, it didn't sound so extreme. Not like his overreacting to someone in his passenger seat.

He supposed they hadn't been in his shoes, either.

"I'll text you his number now. That way you'll have it." She smiled again. "See you at your dad's."

When the door shut, he allowed himself a few minutes of stillness. Brooke was right. The fact he'd been able to idle in the driveway with her in his truck had to count for something. He backed out and flicked on the radio. "I'll Be Home for Christmas" played, and he let out a soft snort.

He was home for Christmas. Brooke had seen for herself his panic attack problem. And oddly, he felt even closer to her because of it. If he could put the accident behind him, his future might look a whole lot brighter.

It was worth a try.

Chapter Nine

Wednesday evening, Brooke nibbled on a frosted sugar cookie in the shape of a bell as she sat in Christy Moulten's living room. For months, Christy had hounded her to join her book club, and in September, Brooke had succumbed to the pressure. To her surprise, she loved the books—they were Christian romance novels with happy endings. This month's selection was a Christmas romance featuring a single dad, his triplet sons and the service dog he hadn't known he'd needed.

Brooke had found the entire thing dreamy. She'd read it in two nights after putting the twins to bed. Both mornings, she'd been groggy, and her leg had been stiff.

Lately, there'd been too many signs in her body telling her she needed to take it easy. But it was Christmas. She finally felt engaged with life, and she didn't want to stay home and rest and keep her stress levels to a minimum.

She wanted to grip life by the horns and take it for a joyride.

"These candles smell sensational." Angela Zane stuck her nose in the candle Brooke had given her when she'd arrived. "I want to gobble it up. So thoughtful of you to make them for us."

"Reagan did everything. I just helped."

"I'm lighting mine as soon as I get home." Mary Corning

selected a gingerbread cookie that sat beside the large frosted brownie on her dessert plate. She craned her neck to the hall. "Where did Reagan go?"

"She had to use the restroom. She'll be right back." Brooke was saving her a seat. Reagan had joined the book club in October after Brooke mentioned how much she enjoyed it.

"I remember those days," Christy said as she carried a tray of mugs into the living room. "My bladder seemed to shrink to the size of a sesame seed when I was pregnant with Cade and Ty."

"Mackenzie isn't coming?" Angela asked.

"No. I keep inviting her. I gave her a copy of the book, but I'll probably have to face the fact she's not into it." Christy handed Brooke a mug of cocoa, then gave one to her best friend, Charlene Parker, who worked at the nursing home in town. "One of these days, I'll wear her down."

Janey Denton, Charlene's daughter, who'd married one of Winston Ranch's cowboys, Lars, in the fall, took a seat on the pale gray couch next to Brooke. Her dessert plate overflowed with various cookies. A woman after her own heart. Reagan returned and promptly took a huge bite of a frosted sugar cookie with red and green sprinkles.

Christy settled into an overstuffed floral chair as Tulip jumped onto the matching ottoman near the fireplace. The little Pomeranian curled up on Christy's lap. Cream-colored quilted stockings hung from the mantel, and the Christmas tree in the corner was decorated with bulbs and ornaments in pastel pinks and greens. Brooke always loved visiting Christy's home, which overflowed with feminine touches.

"Now that everyone's here, we can get started." Christy's eyes glimmered in anticipation. "But first, let's hear the updates. Reagan, how are you feeling?"

Reagan glanced up mid-bite of a cookie. After brushing

crumbs from her lips, she held up a finger and finished chewing. "Great. The first trimester was rough. Now that the nausea has passed, I'm enjoying the pregnancy."

"We can't wait to babysit." Christy pressed her palms together in the prayer position. "Can we, Char?"

"I adore babies." Charlene nodded. "I miss holding Megan and Alice. They're growing up way too quickly."

"I agree," Brooke said. "Every time they go up a size in clothes, I end up crying. I have all their old clothes packed away for the church rummage sale next summer. Unless you have a girl, Reagan, in which case you should take all of them."

"We don't know what we're having. Marc and I decided not to find out." With a loving expression, she rubbed her baby bump. "It'll be a surprise."

As the conversation veered to pros and cons of finding out the gender beforehand, Brooke's mind wandered to last Friday's surprise—sitting in Dean's truck as he dealt with his trauma. Almost immediately, she'd regretted pushing him into letting her get in the truck with him. Seeing how deeply it affected him had broken her heart.

But she'd also sensed how his panic had stolen part of his future. He'd flat-out told her he was staying single because of it. What exactly had he been through the night of the accident to affect him so terribly?

They'd been spending their evenings together, partly because he'd been working on her bathroom, and partly because she insisted he join her and the girls for supper every night. She learned more about him each day, and it was getting harder and harder to avoid her feelings. Dean shared her values. He made her feel safe, smart, important.

"How are the driving lessons with Clem going, Christy?" Mary was the only one in the room who could ask her that with a straight face. Christy was notorious for having her driver's license revoked at least three times a year. Back when she'd announced she was moving to town, Clem had offered to give her lessons. Last Brooke had heard, they weren't going well.

"Not good." Christy took a sip of hot tea. "We took a hiatus for the month of November after he yelled at me for hitting a curb while turning onto Maple Street. I told him there wasn't enough room for my Ford Escape to *not* hit the curb. He claimed that was nonsense, and I told him I wanted to Ford Escape his judgmental tone. Let's just say words were exchanged."

That was putting it mildly, if Brooke had to guess. She'd seen those two get into shouting matches that could go on for days.

"Anyway," Christy continued, "our tempers cooled, and last week he wanted me to drive to Casper to visit Ed. We didn't make it more than two blocks before he started harping on me for not braking soon enough. I didn't know what in the world he was talking about—I brake in plenty of time, and I told him so. Well, he disagreed, and I don't need that kind of negativity in my life, so I pulled into the feed store's parking lot and cut the engine. He claimed I was a menace to society every time I got behind the wheel. I told him he was a menace to society for being alive."

Everyone hung on her words. Anytime a conversation included her driving and/or Clem, it was sure to be entertaining. This one didn't disappoint.

"What happened next?" Janey asked. Her blond hair had been French-braided and tied with a red ribbon. She'd accepted the full-time position of second-grade teacher at the elementary school. To think, it would only be a few years before Megan and Alice went to school. Hopefully, Janey would still be teaching by then.

"He got that hard look in his eyes—you know, the steely one—and told me to hand over my license. I refused."

"Why would he want your license?" Brooke eyed the brownie on her plate. *Yes.* She took a bite.

"He made a scissor-cutting motion with his fingers." Christy widened her eyes and dropped her chin to emphasize her words. A collective gasp filled the room.

"He wouldn't." Charlene shook her head.

"Oh, I think he would." Christy's chin bobbed. "My license stayed tucked into my wallet, where it has remained ever since. Clem ended up driving to Casper and back. We called a truce. Anyway, enough about me. Brooke, how is your bathroom shaping up?"

All eyes turned to her. "It's great. The new vanity door came in on Monday, and Dean and Terry installed the floor tiles this week. They'll be able to finish up by Friday."

"Wonderful news. Just in time for Christmas. I can't believe it's next Wednesday already. How did that happen? Ed sure is thankful Dean stepped in and took over for him."

"I'm thankful, too." Brooke set the brownie back on her plate. "Once the bathroom is done and the back ramp is built, I'll have more peace of mind."

She didn't miss the exchange of glances among the ladies, and she didn't care. They didn't need to understand why the renovations were important to her.

"Speaking of Dean, any chance he'll stick around Jewel River after Ed comes home?" Charlene asked.

"I don't know." Brooke hoped so—more than hoped. She looked forward to each day when he finished whatever was on the agenda for her bathroom. She'd learned a lot about him, and she wanted to learn even more.

"It would be good for Ed to have him around," Angela said. "Then he'll be able to pass on the company to him."

Unless Dean didn't want to take over the company.

"I still don't understand why he quit construction altogether to work on a ranch down in Texas. We have plenty of ranches here if he wanted to work with cattle so bad." Mary shrugged.

Now that Brooke had seen firsthand what Dean had gone through by having her in the passenger seat of his truck, she knew exactly why he'd gotten that job on the ranch in Texas.

His accident had broken something inside him. Just like her stroke had broken something inside her.

"The past is in the past," Janey said. "We can be thankful he's here now."

Brooke's thoughts exactly. But when Ed returned, would Dean stay? He'd made it clear when he first arrived that this was a temporary landing for him. If he didn't settle down in Jewel River, where would he go?

Her appetite fled. She shouldn't have encouraged their friendship to blossom the way it had. Spending all this time with him was a mistake.

At least the basement was almost complete. On Friday, they'd gone through a large amount of the remaining items. Dean had dropped off several boxes to one of the church members who stored items for the church's rummage sale. He'd also taken another truckload of donations to one of the thrift shops in Casper. Without all the boxes and bags clogging up the basement, it looked bigger. The space could be used for something other than a catchall for junk.

There'd been a few times Brooke had caught Dean opening a box only to clench his jaw and pack it up quickly. His mother's things, she supposed. Wasn't any of her business. It did make her question if Dean had unresolved issues from his past, though. Brooke certainly had wounds that hadn't healed from her father's abandonment.

"Let's talk about the book." Christy's cheery tone cut through her thoughts. She turned her attention to the group. "What did you all think about the hero, Rick?"

"I loved him," Janey said. "But Dierdre got on my nerves—at least at first."

"I warmed up to her after the first couple chapters," Reagan added sweetly.

"I couldn't get enough of those triplets," Charlene said. "The only thing that would have improved the book for me, personally, is if Rick had been a cowboy."

"I hear you on that," Brooke said. She pictured Dean in his cowboy boots and Stetson. The way he hefted the boxes in Ed's basement and carried them upstairs as if they weighed less than a bag of marshmallows made her want to fan herself. Yes, give her a cowboy any day.

And that cowboy sure could kiss.

Stop it! That was a onetime kiss.

Onetime kiss or not, Dean was one swoony cowboy, and she'd savor what they had for the moment.

It wouldn't last. But at least she'd have some good memories.

That should do it. Dean finished spray-painting the final circle on the lawn in Brooke's backyard on Friday afternoon. The company had finally made it out yesterday to flag the yard. Now that he knew exactly where the gas and electricity lines ran, he could dig the holes for the new posts. After they thawed the ground.

"Once we get the fires going good, we'll cover them with the metal ovens." Marc pointed to one of the circles. "Needs more kindling. Man, it's cold out here."

Terry wrung old newspaper tightly and stuffed it in between the split logs, where flames sputtered. "My daddy taught me all his campfire tricks. Why, I must have made half a million fires in my sixty-four years…"

Dean glanced at Marc, who pressed his lips together to hide his laughter. Dean had told Marc how well he and Terry got along—except for the age-reference thing. He didn't need any more reminders of Terry's sixty-four years.

"That newspaper trick does seem to be working." Marc pivoted and went to the driveway, where they'd set out the supplies. He came back with one of the old metal pans, some wire mesh and a few large rocks. "Here, why don't you put this over the fire, Terry?"

"Me?" The man grinned. "Sure thing."

Terry took the pan and bent over, his girth straining against his winter coveralls. Then he straightened and nudged it in place with his foot.

"Now what?" Dean asked.

"Mesh. Rocks. Repeat." Marc pointed to the other circles.

It took about an hour to get all the fires started, and once they were done, they went inside. Brooke sat at the kitchen island, sipping something hot from a mug with purple flowers as she read a book.

Dean wouldn't have minded walking into that scene every day for the rest of his life. She glanced up and smiled. "Done already?"

"Not even close." Marc approached and gave her a side hug. "I take it the girls are napping?"

"For another hour."

"You have any more coffee?"

"Fresh pot. Help yourself."

Dean hung back, and Terry asked Marc to pour him a cup, too.

"The tile looks incredible." As she held the mug between her hands, her beauty took his breath away. "Oh, Mom dropped off two dozen doughnuts. She knew you were coming over and said it would make the job go quicker if you had sustenance."

Marc had already opened the box. He chomped half a cruller in one bite and grinned. "She knows me too well." Then he turned to Terry and Dean and tossed each of them a doughnut.

Dean caught his—barely. If he kept this up, he'd have to start jogging or something. His active lifestyle as a ranch hand was a far cry from eating doughnuts and all these delicious suppers with Brooke. The fact her mom dropped off pastries here each day—and that they were the best ones he'd ever eaten in his life—didn't help.

"I'd work any job just for Anne's baked goods," Terry said. "That woman knows how to cook."

"Couldn't agree more." Marc selected a chocolate-covered doughnut. "Want another?"

Terry nodded. Dean shook his head.

"What's the verdict out there?" Brooke's tone was cheerful, but there was a strain in her eyes he wasn't used to seeing. Was she paler than normal? Dean didn't want to stare, but he couldn't help it. He worried about her.

Last Friday's kiss had affected him deeply. He hadn't stopped thinking about it—or her—since.

"Thawing the ground as we speak." Marc took a loud slurp of coffee. "In a couple hours, we can dig the holes and set the posts. We'll have to use the utility sink in the laundry room for hot water to mix the cement."

"Why?" she asked.

"To make sure it sets properly in the cold," Dean explained. "I bought special cement for it."

"Oh, I didn't realize. That makes sense." She nodded. "And then what?"

He had come to know her pretty well over these past weeks. He wanted to go over there, take her hand in his and tell her not to stress out—that he was taking care of everything. But he stayed where he was and let Marc answer.

"Then these guys can get to work building the actual ramp."

"How long will that take?"

"A couple days," Dean said. "But I won't be able to start until Monday. The cement has to cure. We're tenting the area with tarps, and we'll have insulated blankets covering the cement, too."

"Do you think it could possibly be done before Christmas?" Her voice had a wistful quality.

"I'll work on it Christmas Eve if I have to. I want everything to be completely done by Christmas. Dad promised you."

"Yeah, well, he didn't know he'd have a heart attack and be stuck in Casper. I don't want you working on my ramp Christmas Eve and missing out on the holiday."

"I won't be missing out. I'll try to get most of it done on Monday. And if I have to come out Tuesday, I'll make sure it's first thing in the morning."

"You'll join us for the Christmas Eve service that night, right?" she asked.

He hadn't thought that far ahead.

"Of course he's coming to church with us on Christmas Eve," Marc said, shaking his head as if it had been a dumb question. Part of him was relieved that they expected him to be with them, and part of him worried he shouldn't be spending all this time with them.

"He might plan on visiting Ed." She glared at her brother.

"He can do that in the afternoon."

Dean had nothing to add to the conversation. He wasn't

sure how he was spending Christmas Eve yet. He probably should figure it out soon, though, since it was only a few short days away.

"I'll let you guys know after I talk to Dad." Dean stretched his back from side to side. "He was acting like he'd be home before Christmas, but I think it will be another week before they'll release him."

"And then what?" Marc asked.

"I'm not sure. Knowing him, he'll want to pick up right where he left off."

"The doctors won't like that." Brooke frowned.

"Trust me, I know they won't."

"No, I meant, what are you going to do?" Marc asked. "Are you staying in town or moving on?"

Leave it to his best friend to cut right to the heart of the matter. Dean stared at the counter. He didn't know his plans, and this wasn't the time or place to figure them out.

"You should stay," Marc said with a nod.

"I agree." Terry walked his fingers toward the doughnut box and grabbed a cinnamon-sugar twist.

Dean glanced Brooke's way. She watched him with a curious expression.

She made him want to stay. She made him want this— all of it. The job, the friends, the town, the time with her and the twins.

But they both had too many hang-ups, too many obstacles, to pursue a relationship.

"Before I forget," Marc said to Brooke, "do you have that heating pad for Reagan? Her lower back's been aching."

"Yep, let me go get it." She stood and left the room.

Terry asked Marc when the baby was due, and Dean tuned out their conversation. He was almost finished with the basement. One more session and it would be done. As much as he wanted to ask Brooke to join him tonight, he couldn't. Didn't want her overdoing it. Especially this close to Christmas.

And every time he was in the same room as her, he had the urge to kiss her.

No, he'd tackle the rest of the basement on his own. Last Friday, he'd found several of his mother's items in the boxes. The locket was the only thing that bothered him. He still hadn't opened it. He'd dropped the rest of her stuff off at the thrift shop in Casper without a second thought.

Maybe he should open the locket and deal with whatever pain it brought up. Get it over with. Go into next year with some closure.

Next year?

Marc had brought up another thing he'd been avoiding. What was he going to do when Dad came back to town?

"Here you go." Brooke returned and handed Marc the heating pad.

Maybe he should call the counselor Brooke had recommended. Find out if the guy could help him get a new perspective.

"Let's see if the fires are still going." Marc pointed to the door. "I want you to have this ramp done. Then you won't have so far to walk from the garage. I still don't know why they built these houses without attached garages."

"The ramp will be more convenient, for sure." Brooke wrapped her arms around her waist. "But I can't complain. The back porch has only been down for a week."

"You ready, Terry?" Marc asked. "Dean?"

He nodded, moving toward the door, but Brooke stopped him.

"Dean, could you wait a minute? I have a question about the bathroom grout." Her head tilted to the side.

"Sure." He turned to Marc. "I'll be out there in a few."

"Take your time. We've got this under control."

Dean followed her down the hall, trying to remember if any of the grout needed fixing. He'd finished the bathroom last night. Terry had helped him install the mirror and towel bars yesterday, and Dean had stuck around touching up paint and verifying everything was caulked and sealed. It looked great.

Afterward, he'd joined Brooke and the girls for a supper of homemade chicken noodle soup and warm bread. Comfort food with the most comforting woman he'd ever met. They'd talked about everything and nothing for hours.

Brooke stopped inside the bathroom and spun to face him. "I know this is weird timing—and it doesn't have to do with my bathroom or the grout, which is perfect, by the way—but Marc brought up something we haven't discussed. What *are* you going to do after Ed comes home?"

"I don't know."

"You don't know, or you don't want to tell me?" An air of dejection covered her. All because of him. "Never mind. It's none of my business."

Now he felt like a jerk. "It is your business."

"No, it's not. You're almost done with my house, and you don't owe me anything. You never did." The words came out tight, practically strangled.

"Hey, I don't mean to sound gruff." She was swiping imaginary dust from the new countertop. He gently turned her to face him. "I owe you a lot."

"No, you don't." She swallowed, still not meeting his gaze. "It's just…"

When she didn't finish the thought, he caressed her upper arms. "Just what?"

"Things in my life happen all of a sudden. It's boring, boring, same-old, same-old, and then wham! When Marc asked about your plans, it hit me that you might not be here much longer." Her big eyes, filled with vulnerability, lifted to his. He wanted to reassure her that he wasn't going anywhere. That nothing had to change. But he couldn't.

"I'm not leaving tonight," he said.

"I know. But the next couple of days will fly by, and then Christmas will be here, and your dad will return, and—" She held her breath.

"And what?"

"And what if I wake up one day and you're gone? Without a goodbye?"

He took her in his arms, wrapping his hands behind her lower back, and stared into her eyes. "I wouldn't leave without saying goodbye."

"You might."

"I won't."

"You can't promise that. You are leaving, aren't you?" Tears began to pool in her eyes, and he almost told her he'd stay forever if she wouldn't cry.

"I don't know, Brooke." Frustration began to build—not at her, but at himself. "If I do leave, I'll say goodbye."

"Ross didn't." She brought her hand to her mouth as if she hadn't expected that to come out of it.

"Is that what this is about?" His frustration vanished like mist in the morning. He brought her closer and held her, letting his cheek rest against her hair. "I'm not going to be killed in action."

"I know. I'm not being logical." She snuggled in closer. "But it's hard. Being the one left behind is hard. Picking up the pieces without any warning is something I never want to go through again."

"You think there would be pieces to pick up if I left?"

She pushed at his chest. "How can you say that? Of course

there would be. I've grown close to you. And you've grown close to me. Don't try to deny it."

He wouldn't. Couldn't. He'd grown very close to her. So close, he was actually considering staying in Jewel River. Working with his dad. Pretending he didn't have an anger issue that almost killed his ex-girlfriend.

Brooke deserved someone better than him.

He sighed. "I don't have my life figured out. I don't know what next year holds. But I promise you this—I'm not taking it lightly, and you will be the first to know when I do figure it out."

She searched his eyes for a few moments and then nodded.

"I'm not being fair to you," she said.

"How so?"

"I want you to stay, but my mind hasn't changed about marriage."

"Are you sure it's your fear of having another stroke holding you back?" After her reaction to the thought of him leaving without saying goodbye, he had a feeling her stance on marriage had more to do with Ross's sudden death than anything else.

"I'm sure." She stepped back, out of his embrace, leaving his hands feeling empty. "What else would it be?"

Dean was no therapist, and it wasn't his place to share his theory.

"What about you?" she asked. "Is your fear of driving with me in the car the only thing that's holding you back?"

"Yes." The hair on the back of his neck stood at attention. What was she getting at?

His mother's locket came to mind. What did that have to do with this? Nothing.

"If you say so." Her lips set in a firm line.

"Maybe in time we'll both get more rational about our

fears." Before the words left his mouth, he knew it was the wrong thing to say.

"Rational?" She blinked a few times. "What's irrational about acknowledging my risk for a stroke?"

"Nothing." He looked around the bathroom with its lowered sink, special commode and grab bars. She followed his gaze.

"Oh, I see." Her inhalation through her nose was loud. "You think all of this is me overreacting."

"I didn't say that."

"You didn't have to. Your traveling eyes said it all." She pushed past him and out of the bathroom.

"Brooke, wait." He hurried out of the room after her, but she didn't stop until she got to the living room.

She turned to him, trembling with emotion. "I know what everyone thinks. I hear what they say. It's all, 'Oh, Brooke's being super cautious,' or 'Wheelchair-accessible? She's taking it a little too far.' But you don't know. None of you were there. I collapsed in front of my three-month-old babies, Dean. If my mom hadn't been there, I probably would have died. She got me to the clinic. They rushed me in the ambulance to Casper. And my life completely changed. So if you have a problem with me preparing my house in case it happens again—which it very well could—tell me now. Get it off your chest. Because this—" she waved wildly to take in the house "—isn't going away. This is my life. And I'm not putting you or any other man through it."

Regret sank down deep inside of him. She was right. And he didn't know what to say. Didn't know how to fix it.

So he did the only thing he could think of. He took her in his arms, looked into her beautiful big eyes, and whispered that he was sorry.

The fear and anger in them disappeared. He cupped her

face in his hands and gently kissed her. "I'm sorry for making you feel that way. What you and I have is all new for me, and I'm terrible at this."

"At what?" Her face twisted in question.

"At women. Relationships. I don't know what I'm doing."

"Yeah, well, I don't know what I'm doing, either." Her mouth curved into a smile. "I guess we'll have to figure it out together. Because I can't seem to stay away from you."

His thoughts exactly.

The front door opened. "Hey, Dean?" Marc hollered. "Did you get lost?"

Dean shook his head, giving her a smile. "That's my cue."

She nodded, the sparkle in her eyes returning.

As he strode to the door, hope filled him. Brooke felt something more for him, too. And they might both be messed up, but at least they weren't hiding from whatever was brewing between them.

But if it ended badly…maybe it would be better if they did.

Chapter Ten

"Meggie, hand me the sprinkles." Monday morning, Brooke held out her hand to Megan, who clutched a plastic tube of red nonpareils. If that child dumped out the container, Brooke was going to lose it. Her patience was already whisker-thin.

Megan's big eyes didn't waver as she slowly shook her head and stood in the space where the kitchen met the living room.

"Give them to Mommy." She thrust her hand closer to the pudgy fingers gripping the tube.

Again, the shaking of the head. These little twins were cute and all, but they were also stubborn. And both were trying her self-control something fierce today. It was terrible timing, too, since she'd felt unwell when she'd woken, which had been an hour earlier than usual.

Her stomach kept churning, and the coffee she'd brewed earlier tasted bitter. Plus, her leg muscles felt weak again.

Megan backed up a few steps. That did it.

"I said, give them here." Brooke reached out and grabbed the tube.

"No, Mama!" Megan began to cry, which only added to the incessant noise of hammering and nail guns pounding from out back. True to his word, Dean had shown up at the crack of dawn to begin installing the boards for the ramp. Each *pop* of the nail gun drilled into her head.

Maybe she should sit on the couch for a while.

The kitchen island held freshly baked cookies, bowls of colored icings, wax paper and several options for sprinkles. She'd promised the girls they'd decorate Christmas cookies, and she doubted she'd have more energy later. Best to do it now.

She spotted Alice licking a full spoon of icing. "Alice! No!"

The child dropped the spoon—icing splattering on the floor—and her lips began to wobble. Then she started wailing even louder than Megan. Soon, both of them were crying at the top of their lungs.

It was times like this she missed living with her mother. At least she'd gotten a break when Mom came home. Now? The only break she could count on was during their naps or after she put them to bed.

Brooke couldn't call any of her family to come over and help out, either. Mom, Marc and Reagan had gone into Casper for some last-minute Christmas shopping and a movie. Both her mother and Reagan had scheduled part-time employees to run their shops today. Neither was in the habit of taking vacations or even the occasional day off. They deserved a day on the town.

After inhaling a deep breath, Brooke went over to Alice, still sobbing, and gave her a hug. Then she bent to pick up the spoon. A light-headed feeling flooded her, and as she straightened, she grew dizzy and grabbed hold of the corner of the counter until it passed.

Not now. Tomorrow was Christmas Eve, and she had so much to do still.

The list of symptoms to watch out for ticked through her mind. Had she eaten? A few bites of toast counted, right? She simply couldn't stomach much at the moment. What about water? Was she hydrated?

Maybe that was her problem. She took a glass from the cupboard and filled it with water from the dispenser in the refrigerator door. For weeks, she'd been telling herself to slow down. But she hadn't.

Megan sniffled her way over to her with Alice not far behind. Brooke took a long drink and set the glass down, then forced a smile and a chipper tone. "Let's decorate the cookies."

To her ears, her voice sounded far away. She nudged the girls toward the hall. "But first, we need to wash up."

"No!" Alice scrunched her face and stamped one foot. Megan copied her.

"We're cleaning our hands. Then we'll decorate the cookies." She didn't want to decorate the cookies. She didn't want to wrestle the girls over to the bathroom sink to wash their hands.

She wanted to go straight to her room, climb into bed and curl up in her softest blanket for a long, long nap.

By the time she'd helped them wash and dry their hands and gotten them situated at their little table, a dull ache filled her head. After spreading out a small tablecloth and putting bibs on both girls, she brought over two paper plates with cutout cookies and handed them each a small silicone spatula. She set three bowls of icing in the center.

The girls happily spread icing over the cookies. Globs of it landed next to the plates.

Oh, well. She smiled as they shook sprinkles over the cookies. Both girls licked their spatulas and dunked them into the bowls. *Mental note: throw all the icing away and only let the girls eat the cookies they were decorating.*

She was still tired, and the dizzy feeling from earlier returned. But now the dull ache in her head was intensifying, too.

The girls were a mess. They had icing and sprinkles all over their faces and hands. But they sure looked happy.

"You can each have one cookie. Then we need to get cleaned up again." Again, the words sounded strange to her ears, like they'd been spoken from far away. She sat on a stool at the island and covered her face with her hands.

She didn't feel good.

The back door opened, and she barely registered the blast of cold air that accompanied Dean. "Check it out. The ramp boards are all in, and one side of the rail is finished. I'll have this done in no time."

"I'll be there" was all she could say. Little lights flashed to her left. Did Dean have a strobe light on or something? "Clean girls."

"What?" He stripped his gloves off as Megan and Alice came at him with their arms in the air. "Oh, you two are sticky. Why don't I help?"

Brooke was vaguely aware of him taking off their bibs. They giggled as they followed him to the kitchen sink. She heard water rushing, more giggles.

A fuzzy filter seemed to cover her eyes. She couldn't see very well. Couldn't think. She was tired. So tired.

And afraid.

"Hey, are you all right?" Dean's voice was near.

Whatever she replied came out garbled. She only had one clear thought.

The doctor.

She needed a doctor.

"Doctor. Call." She pointed…somewhere.

"The doctor?" His strong arm went around her shoulders. "Here, lean against me. I'll help you to the living room."

When she barely moved, he swung her into his arms and carried her to the couch. She could sense the darkness slipping in. Could feel her body refusing to obey as she rested there. The fear grew into something worse.

"Muh phone." She lifted her arm, her finger, to the ceiling.

Seconds later, her phone was in her hands. She tried to press the buttons but couldn't.

"Doctor," she said.

"You need the doctor. Okay." He sounded worried.

Even in her groggy state, her mind warned her this was the stroke she'd feared. The one she'd known would come. She just wished it wasn't happening so soon.

Think, Dean.

Something was wrong with Brooke. Very wrong. Her phone slipped out of her fingers and fell to the floor with a thud. The twins stood on either side of him, poking Brooke's arm and repeating, "Mama?"

"Let's give your mom a little space." He pulled out his phone and found the number for the clinic. They answered on the first ring. Relief made him raise his face to the ceiling, until he realized it was an automated system. He pressed one for the receptionist. Two for an appointment. And the dreaded instrumental music began to play.

Maybe he should call 911. He padded over to Brooke, took her hand in his and squeezed it. It was cool to the touch. She moaned and turned onto her side toward the back of the couch. He felt her forehead. Normal temperature. Tried to take her pulse, but he'd never been good at it. Was it too fast? Too slow? He didn't know. Finally, someone at the clinic picked up.

"Hi, something's wrong with my friend." *My friend?* Moron. Brooke was way more than a friend. "She's slurring her words, really tired—"

The receptionist asked him several questions. He was

wasting time. "No, she's not under the influence of alcohol. She's a mom with twin girls…yes, it's Brooke." The woman advised him to call an ambulance. "Okay, I'll call them now."

He ended the call and dialed 911. The operator informed him the nearest ambulance was half an hour away. Thirty minutes? Way too long. He hung up, and worry spun inside him.

Now what?

If Anne or Marc were here, they'd drive her to the clinic. But they weren't here. And Brooke clearly needed medical attention ASAP.

What if this *was* a stroke? What if she died? What if he was waiting too long right now and she ended up paralyzed?

He had to drive her to the clinic. Him. His breathing came in shallow gasps.

The twins were watching him, wide-eyed. He would *not* be responsible for these precious babies losing their mother.

"Brooke?" He gave her shoulder a gentle shake. She groaned. "Brooke? Can you hear me?"

She gave no indication she'd heard him.

He knew what he had to do, but he didn't know if he could do it.

God, don't ask this of me. Help me!

"Come on, girls," he said, choking on the words. "We're getting our coats on. Taking a drive."

They climbed down and scampered to him. Their lips were wobbling as if ready to cry. He knew the feeling. If he wasn't so stressed, he'd want to cry, too.

"Where are your coats and boots?" he asked. They ran toward the hallway closet. He followed and helped them into their outerwear, then grabbed Brooke's winter coat and rooted around the floor for a pair of her shoes. Then he went back to the couch and eased her into a seated position.

"I need your help, Brooke. I'm taking you to the clinic. Help me get your arm into the coat, okay?" He used his gentlest voice, and it cracked with fear. At least she wasn't unconscious. She moved her arm as he asked. "Good. Now let's get your other one in there."

After placing a shoe on each foot, he left her on the couch and picked up the twins to carry them to her minivan. The cold air hadn't bothered him earlier, but it felt frigid now. He buckled Megan into her seat and Alice into hers, and promised them he'd be right back. Inside, he found Brooke's phone and cradled her in his arms, snatching up her purse on his way out. He got her settled into the passenger seat, buckled her seat belt and rushed around to the driver's side. Rooted around in the purse for her keys. Found them and started the minivan.

As soon as the engine came to life, his world seemed to retreat into slow motion. Snow had begun to fall, and he could make out each snowflake as it hit the windshield. The girls were silent in the back seat. Christmas music played on the radio. The wipers swished back and forth.

He glanced at Brooke—out of it. Lethargic. His body froze harder than the ground he'd had to thaw with Marc's and Terry's help. Except there wasn't a metal oven to thaw him. Nothing would fix this.

Drive!

His brain yelled one thing, but his body refused. His mind flashed back to the wreckage from a decade ago, this time with visions of Brooke mangled next to him. And the twins.

His throat tightened to the point he was choking. His eyes bugged out, and he tore at the zipper at his collar.

He couldn't breathe. Couldn't move. Couldn't drive.

He couldn't go through with this.

"Dee?" one of the twins asked.

He snapped out of it, blinking, gulping deep breaths, but still not getting enough air.

"Yes?" He tried to sound normal.

"Mama?"

"I'm taking care of it, darlin'."

Lord, I need Your strength. I've tried this before and failed every single time. I've failed at so many things in my life. Please, have mercy on me. I don't deserve it, but Brooke does. Get us to the clinic safely. I'm begging You!

He swallowed bile, clenched his jaw and put the minivan into Reverse.

"We're taking your mama to see the doctor." He'd never backed out of a driveway slower in his life. His hands shook. His stomach rolled. But he kept going. And when he reached the end of her drive, he waited twice as long as he normally would to make sure no cars were coming. By the time he actually pulled onto the street, his palms were slick with sweat. If he hadn't been choking on fear, he probably would have been crying.

He was a broken man.

The speedometer showed the van traveling at a solid seventeen miles per hour. He didn't even attempt to go faster. He still couldn't catch his breath. He needed to keep his eyes on the road and continue driving. All that mattered was getting Brooke to the clinic. Safely. In one piece. Without smashing the minivan into a pole or a tree and crumpling it up.

The closer they got to the clinic, the easier he found it to breathe. He checked the twins in the rearview—they weren't crying. That had to count for something. His palms weren't slick with sweat anymore, either.

The clinic's parking lot came into view, and the relief flowing through his veins overwhelmed him. Just a little farther... The van crawled into the lot, and he eased into a parking space. Cut the engine. Let his head fall back against the headrest, and closed his eyes for the briefest of moments. *Thank You, Jesus. Please, don't let me be too late.*

Now what? He couldn't carry Brooke *and* the twins. Did he leave them out here alone? He was going to have to. Brooke's health was the priority.

"I'll be right back to get you two, okay?" They both nodded. Then he got out, hurried to the passenger side, unbuckled the seat belt and swung Brooke into his arms. Using his hip, he closed the door and power walked the short distance to the entrance. Two wheelchairs were inside, and he placed her in one and wheeled her to the reception window.

"Hello?" No one was there. He pounded on the small bell on the counter. *Ding! Ding! Ding!*

A young woman in scrubs appeared. "May I help you?"

"Brooke—she needs medical help. The ambulance was thirty minutes out, so I brought her here."

"You did the right thing." The woman sprang into action, yelling for one of the nurses to get the doctor. Then she came through the door and wheeled Brooke away, calling over her shoulder, "Don't go far! We need to ask you questions."

"Give me a minute. I have to get the twins." There was so much he wanted to say to Brooke. So many things he hadn't realized until this moment. But the twins were alone in the minivan, and Brooke had already disappeared from view.

He raced outside and slid open the van door. Both girls appeared to be on the verge of tears.

"Hey, there, I'm back. We're going inside to wait for your mama, okay?"

"Mama?" Alice's watery blue eyes stared up at him.

"Yep, she's inside, sweetheart."

He unbuckled them from their car seats. Snow landed on their hoods as he made his way to the entrance. Inside, a nurse was waiting for him. She asked about Brooke's symptoms as he helped the girls get their coats off. When he'd answered all her questions, he led them over to a children's table with crayons and coloring sheets.

They showed no interest in coloring, and instead lifted their arms for him to pick them up. Glancing around, he spotted a stack of children's picture books. He snagged one and sat down, then boosted the twins onto his lap.

"I'll read you a story, but first I need to call your uncle." He gave each of them what he hoped passed for a smile. Then he slipped his phone out of his pocket and found Marc's number. It rang twice, and Marc answered.

"Hey, Marc, we have a bit of a situation here."

"What are you talking about?" His tone went from relaxed to tense instantly.

"Brooke wasn't feeling good, so I took her to the clinic."

The line was silent for two beats. "Define not feeling good."

His chest seemed to be snagged with briars as he tried to form the words. "Tired, slurring her words, unaware of her surroundings."

Marc hissed something Dean couldn't make out.

"What are the doctors saying?" Marc asked.

"Nothing yet. We just arrived."

"We?"

"Yeah, I've got the girls."

"Oh, man, thanks. Just a sec." Dean could hear Marc telling Reagan and his mom what was going on.

"Dean? Describe what happened." Anne must have grabbed Marc's phone. In the background, Marc was protesting for her to give it back. Dean told her exactly what he told Marc. "She didn't pass out?"

"No."

"Did one side of her face seem to freeze? And did you notice if she could move her limbs?"

"Her face seemed normal. I don't know about her limbs. I think she could move them. She did move her arms. She seemed more weak and out of it than anything." The temptation to rake his fingers through his hair grew strong, but he couldn't with the twins on his lap.

"Good. That's good." Anne's voice grew muffled as she relayed what he'd said to Marc and Reagan. "Listen, we'll come home now. I'll call Christy Moulten to take care of the twins."

"I'm not going anywhere." His tone grew firm. "I'm staying right here with these two until I know what's happening with Brooke."

"Thank you, Dean," Anne's voice softened. "We'll be there in an hour and a half. Sooner if Marc has anything to do with it."

"I'll keep you posted with any updates."

They ended the call. He kept an eye on the receptionist window and the door leading to the examination rooms. What was happening? Was Brooke okay? He wished someone would come out and explain everything to him.

Alice held the book he'd selected. He might as well keep the girls entertained and calm while he waited.

"This looks good," he said. "I like Christmas and polar bears."

As he began to read, the girls snuggled into his sides. They made him want to protect them from everything life would throw their way, including what was happening to their mommy.

He'd let the doctors take care of Brooke. And in the meantime, he'd take care of her girls. It was the least he could do for the woman who'd brought him back to life.

Chapter Eleven

"How are you feeling?" A man's voice cut through the fog in her brain. Brooke forced her eyes open.

The crinkle of paper as she shifted on the examination table alerted her that she was at the doctor's office. An IV was hooked up to her arm. Dread poisoned her veins.

Was it another stroke?

Her head ached, and the grogginess from earlier lingered. She gingerly wriggled her fingers, toes, legs and arms. She could feel and move every part of her body! The realization almost brought her to tears.

"What happened?" Her throat was parched.

Dr. South handed her a small cup of water. She drank it in one gulp. Better.

"Dean McCaffrey brought you in about twenty minutes ago. He was concerned about your symptoms." Dean? That couldn't be right. He didn't drive with other people in his vehicle. "The ambulance will be here shortly to take you to Casper for further testing."

"Further testing?" She brought the hand not hooked up to the IV to her chest. "Was it…? Did I…?"

"Have a stroke?" he added.

She nodded.

"I don't think so. We took your vitals, and once we got the IV started, you rebounded pretty quickly. I'm not ruling one out, though, given your history. You need testing we don't have here. Do you remember anything from before Dean brought you in?"

Her mom. Marc and Reagan. They were shopping.

The twins. Who had the girls?

"My girls?"

"With Dean in the waiting room." His patient smile reassured her. "Nurse Jody's out there playing peekaboo and giving them animal crackers. You know she dotes on them."

Of course. No one in Jewel River would let the twins be alone. Why had she even considered it? Everyone in this community had helped with Megan and Alice at some point in their almost two years of life. It humbled her. Filled her with gratitude. She had a lot of thank-you prayers to offer God later.

"Back to earlier," Dr. South said. "What do you remember?"

"Cookies." She remembered being mad at Megan for stealing the sprinkles. And then at Alice for licking the spoonful of icing. "We were supposed to decorate cookies, and I was tired and nauseous. I felt off."

"Mmm-hmm." He typed on his laptop. "Go on."

"I let the girls frost the cookies, and I thought I'd better have some water. So I did. Then I saw little lights."

"Flashing lights?"

"Yes."

"On one side or everywhere?"

"One side."

The clickity-clack of his fingers typing filled the room. "And then?"

"Dean came inside. He's been finishing the ramp out back. I told him to call the doctor."

"I see."

"Everything's fuzzy from that point on. I felt so tired, and my head hurt. I wanted to close my eyes and rest. I… I don't remember much after that."

He stopped typing and met her gaze. "I suspect you had a migraine with aura. When you get to Casper and have the tests, they'll be able to give you an accurate diagnosis. You've had all of them before, so you know the drill. In my professional opinion, I don't think this episode is as serious as it appears."

Not serious? Was he joking?

"You told me the signs to watch for in case of a stroke. All the signs were there." She ticked through the list in her head. Well, not all of them.

"Migraines can be mistaken for strokes. Both share a lot of attributes. I don't think you need to worry."

"All I do is worry." Had she really said that out loud?

"I understand. It's reasonable, given your circumstances. I hope, in time, you won't worry so much."

"I don't see my anxiety levels changing anytime soon." She wanted to hug herself, but the IV line was in her way. "I could have a stroke at any moment."

He gave her a kind look. "You do have an increased risk, but it's not as high as you might think. You don't have the most common risk factors. Your blood pressure is normal, your cholesterol levels are great, you're at a healthy weight, and you're young."

"Yes, but I had a stroke before. And even if this was a migraine, doesn't that increase my risk, too?" She had memorized the literature. Knew all the risk factors. Understood she didn't have the typical ones that caused a stroke.

What did it matter? She'd had a stroke less than two years ago, and she'd been young. Too young. Why did what happened today not count?

"I wish someone could give me an answer. Do I have a

fifty percent higher chance of having another stroke? Seventy-five? I feel like I'm walking on eggshells, waiting to be paralyzed or worse."

She hadn't realized how keyed up she was, how much worry and tension she'd been holding inside, until all of that came out.

"Fifty? Seventy-five? No." Frowning, he shook his head. "Not even close."

What had her neurologist told her? The last time she'd gotten a follow-up checkup had been in June, a year after the stroke. She'd heard *increased risk* and assumed the worst.

"Then what is it? My neurologist has told me time and again that, compared to the average person, I have an increased risk of having a stroke. All the research I've done has confirmed it, and you've said it, too."

"You're right. I can't give you an exact number, but I can tell you it's well below the percentages you mentioned. About one in four people who've had a stroke end up having another one. That includes the most at-risk group—older people. You're managing your risk factors well. I'd place you well below twenty-five percent."

"It feels like the threat is always there, waiting to take me down."

"It's normal to feel that way, but our fears don't necessarily reflect reality."

"What if I get to the hospital, and it wasn't a migraine? What if I *did* have another stroke?" Tears pooled in her eyes.

"Then it's a good thing Dean got you here when he did, because you're sitting here talking to me, and that's a good sign."

A knock on the door drew their attention. "The ambulance is here."

"Send them in." Dr. South nodded.

"Can I see the girls?"

He hesitated. "I'll have Nurse Jody bring them in—just for a moment, though."

"Can Dean come, too?" She needed to see him. Needed to verify he'd brought her here. Needed to make sure he could take care of her babies until arrangements were made.

"Briefly."

Had he really driven her here? She couldn't imagine how difficult that must have been for him.

Her head still ached, but she didn't dare close her eyes. Was it wishful thinking to believe Dr. South's conclusion that she'd had a migraine? The symptoms screamed stroke to her.

Seconds later, Dean walked in with the twins and her purse.

"Mama!" They both twisted in his arms to reach for her. She attempted a smile as she shook her head.

"I can't hold you right now, my loves. I will as soon as I can, though, I promise." She met Dean's gaze. His eyes were full of concern, hope—and something more.

That glimpse of the depth of his feelings scared her. She couldn't offer him forever. She wasn't even sure she'd have tomorrow. Look at her current situation.

"Are you okay?" he asked. Megan whined as she reached for Brooke. He kept his hold on the girls as he let the purse drop from his hand onto Brooke's lap. "I figured you'd need this."

"Thanks. I think I'm okay. They're taking me to Casper for tests."

"Was it a stroke?"

She wasn't going to lie to him. "They aren't sure. The doctor thinks it was a migraine. But...I don't know."

He nodded. Nurse Jody pulled on Dean's sleeve. "Time's up."

The medics stood in the doorway. "Excuse me, but we need to get in there."

"I'll follow you to Casper with the girls." Dean stepped closer to the bed.

"No, I want them home. The tests take forever." Brooke took Megan's hand and squeezed it, then did the same with Alice's. "Be good for Dean. Mommy loves you. I'll see you soon. Dean, did you call my mom? Oh, and call Christy. She'll take care of the girls."

He nodded. "I'll drive to the hospital later—alone."

"Please don't." She hated seeing the hurt in his eyes, but there was no point in him driving all that way. "I'll be getting tests done, and you won't be able to see me."

With pain in his eyes, he backed up and left the room as the twins started to cry. The sound tore at her heart. Their cries faded as the medics prepared to load her into the ambulance. Minutes later, as they shut the ambulance's doors and the sirens started, she closed her eyes.

Maybe this really had been just a migraine. But what would happen next time?

She hated living in constant fear like this. She'd never put Dean through a lifetime with her health problems. She wasn't enough. Not for an amazing guy like him.

After getting the girls buckled into their car seats, Dean prepared himself for another panic attack. So far, no gasping of breath. He glanced at the passenger seat. Didn't see visions of wreckage. No mangled metal or crumpled bodies. All he saw was an empty seat.

He wished it wasn't empty. Wanted Brooke there with him.

He started the minivan. *Now* the panic attack would begin. He waited for the symptoms. At least this time he knew it was possible for him to drive through them. Honestly, he hadn't acknowledged what a triumph that was until this moment.

He'd done it. He'd driven Brooke and the girls—and he'd

been breathless, with sweaty palms, a tight chest and the terrifying feeling that he was going to die or kill them. And they'd all survived.

Oh, God, You are good. You alone got us to the clinic. Thank You!

While the engine warmed, he called Marc to give him the update. In the background, Anne told Marc to turn around and head back to Casper. They were meeting Brooke at the hospital.

With that out of the way, he shifted the van into Reverse. His heart pumped faster, and his breathing quickened.

None of it was a surprise. These were the symptoms he knew and loathed.

What did it matter, though? He forced himself to inhale. Exhaled slowly. Repeated it. He couldn't breathe deeply, but he could breathe.

God had given him the strength to get Brooke and the girls to the clinic safely. Dean could count on Him to help him get the twins back to her house.

With moist palms and adrenaline rushing through his body, he backed out of the parking spot. Took his time turning onto Center Street. Tried not to think about his tight chest or the difficulty he was having with his breathing.

Last-minute Christmas shoppers clutched scarves as they ducked in and out of shops. If anyone noticed the minivan crawling at eighteen miles per hour, they didn't seem to care.

He was doing this. Again. Driving with passengers in the car. Sure, he hadn't cracked twenty miles per hour, but who cared? It wasn't perfect, and it didn't have to be.

He just needed to get them home safely.

Brooke's street was up ahead, and he slowed even more. Why didn't Brooke want him at the hospital with her? Didn't he mean anything to her? Didn't she want him by her side?

They'd gotten close. Only a few days ago, she'd clung to him, asking him to at least say goodbye before he left.

Maybe that was the problem. He hadn't made her any promises beyond assuring her he'd say goodbye if he left.

Did he want to leave?

No. He wanted more. Wanted long-term. Wanted Brooke.

For a decade, he'd cut himself off from relationships beyond short visits and texts with Marc and his father. But his time in Jewel River had shown him he could have more.

It's not for you to decide. Brooke isn't getting remarried. Period. And she made it clear that she doesn't need you the way you need her.

Dean pulled into her driveway, parked and carried the twins up the front porch. Christy Moulten, shivering in a parka with a furry hood, stood on the welcome mat, waiting for him.

"Anne called." Her kind smile brimmed with compassion. "I'll take care of these little dears until we know more."

"I can take care of them if you have somewhere else you need to be." He gave a slight nod to the front door. "It's unlocked. Didn't have time to lock it earlier." He'd been too busy having a mental breakdown over the realization he had to drive Brooke to the clinic.

"It will be hours before they come back. This is where I need to be." Her understanding tone took the edge off his raw emotions. "I'm so glad you were here."

She opened the door and waited for him to carry in the twins before closing it. Together they peeled off the girls' coats and boots. He left his own on. Figured he might as well finish the ramp's railing while there was daylight. At least he'd be able to keep his promise to Brooke that her projects would be completed before Christmas.

It would also mean he wouldn't have a reason to come back.

But that was okay. He didn't belong here anyway.

"Come on, girls, you look like you need some milk and cookies." Christy took them by their little hands and walked down the hallway to the kitchen. With a glance over her shoulder, she included Dean. "You look like you need some, too."

He wanted to decline, but her tone left no room for argument, so he joined them in the kitchen.

"What happened?" She found two sippy cups and a glass from one of the cupboards, then took out a gallon of milk from the fridge and poured. Handed each of the twins a sippy cup and guided them to the living room couch.

He took his milk with him and sat in one of the chairs while Christy settled on the couch with Megan on one side of her and Alice on the other. The girls could barely keep their eyes open while they drank their milk.

As Dean filled her in on the events of the day, Christy nodded thoughtfully. "I see God's hand in this. Just think what might have happened if you weren't here. With Anne and Marc and Reagan in Casper, who else could have taken her to the clinic? I couldn't have driven them. I still have two more weeks on a suspended license. What a blessing you are to all of us, Dean."

He frowned, not expecting those words to come out of her mouth.

"You've been an answer to so many people's prayers," she said. "Ed's, for sure, since he's been recovering. But Brooke's, too. You have no idea how important it was for her to have everything in here accessible for a wheelchair. And can you blame her? Look at today. It's a good thing she's not suffering any ill effects, whether it was a migraine or not."

He finished his milk, not knowing what to say.

"Patrick and I had lunch at Dixie B's last week," she said.

"He raved about the work you're doing for his service dog training center. He can't believe how quickly the work is getting done, and the quality of it, too…"

As Christy went on about the pole barn he'd finished, Dean's mind wandered. She was making him see himself in a new light. A good light. One he hadn't seen himself in for a long time. Maybe ever.

"…and it's not every day a single cowboy like yourself could handle getting toddler twins buckled into their car seats and off to the clinic while taking care of their mother…"

If only Christy had any idea how hard it had actually been—the panic, the desperation he felt having to drive those three to the clinic. Brooke, Megan and Alice—treasures, each one. His treasures.

God, I love them. He almost gasped. Kept his face schooled and nodded as Christy talked on and on.

He loved Brooke. He loved her twins.

And she didn't love him back. Didn't want him around for moral support.

"Listen, I'm going to finish up the railing on the ramp out back." He stood abruptly. "It shouldn't be more than an hour. I'll try to keep as quiet as possible. Then I'm taking off. Holler if you need me."

The girls were almost asleep. Christy beamed at him. "You are too good to be true. Thank you."

He crossed over and kissed the top of Alice's head, then Megan's, and he thanked Christy before letting himself out. For the next hour, he forced all thoughts out of his head to focus on finishing the rail. Then he loaded his materials into the truck and drove straight to Moulten Stables.

He'd never needed a long ride on Dusty more than he did this minute. After methodically saddling the horse, he led him outside. Dusty shook his mane and snorted, clearly eager to get out and stretch his legs. Soon Dean was in the saddle, and they headed through the snow toward the trails leading to the back of the property.

What was he supposed to do?

He loved Brooke, and there was no way he'd be able to convince her she wouldn't have another stroke. For all he knew, she'd had one today. When he thought about her so lethargic and incoherent and tired, it was all he could do to keep it together.

Dusty picked up the pace as they entered the woods. Though it looked like a winter wonderland, he couldn't enjoy it.

Christy's words from earlier ran through his mind. *I see God's hand in this.*

He saw God's hand in it, too. Dean had been able to drive Brooke when he hadn't been able to drive anyone for years.

God had made the impossible possible.

Lord, thank You, again, for getting us to the clinic safely. Thank You for helping me push through the panic when Brooke needed me the most. I don't know what would have happened if You hadn't gotten me through it.

The verse he loved came back—*I can do all things through Christ.*

Yes, he could.

He *could* drive with other people in the vehicle without crashing it and hurting them. He *had* come through for Brooke when she'd needed him most. And he'd kept his promise to finish her remodeling projects.

He'd taken a huge step forward in his personal life today.

There was one more promise he wanted to keep. With a click of his tongue, he turned Dusty back toward the stables.

Dad's basement still had a few piles to dispose of. He

could get it done tonight. And later, he needed closure on something else.

The locket.

By ten that evening, Brooke had officially been discharged from the hospital in Casper. As her mom harassed a nurse about what she could or could not do for the next few days, she sat in the wheelchair the hospital insisted on. Reagan stood next to her and held her hand.

"Praise God, praise God…" Reagan kept saying under her breath.

Brooke wasn't as elated as Reagan. She probably should have been, but getting discharged didn't change her situation.

After performing a slew of tests, the doctors concluded what Dr. South had suspected. No stroke, but a migraine with aura. A particularly bad migraine, at that.

The doctor had written a prescription for medicine to take whenever she had migraine-like symptoms to stop the attack in its tracks. And she'd had an in-depth discussion with the neurologist about her fears. Like Dr. South, this doctor seemed to think her chances of having another stroke were much lower than she believed.

As much as she wanted to trust that the doctors were right, a little voice in her head told her she couldn't.

She never should have had the first stroke. How could anyone claim she wasn't likely to have another?

Marc pulled the truck to a stop near the sliding glass doors, and Brooke pushed herself out of the wheelchair. Reagan reached over to help her. She was tempted to fling her arm away and hiss that she could manage on her own. But shame filled her at the thought. Reagan was the most supportive person she'd ever met.

Brooke would not hurt her feelings. She'd hurt enough

feelings for one day. Every time she recalled the look on Dean's face as he'd carried the twins out of the examination room, her heart twisted.

"I can manage." Brooke attempted to smile, but it felt tighter than the skinny jeans she'd worn in high school.

"Let her help, Brooke." Mom sounded exasperated. "I had the nurse call in the prescription to the pharmacy back home. We'll have to pick it up early tomorrow. I'm sure they're closing by noon, with it being Christmas Eve and all." She blocked Brooke's path. "Where are you going? You're not sitting in the back. You're up front with Marc. The back seat is notorious for car sickness, and you've been through enough for one day."

She'd gotten rid of the migraine, but her mom's fussing might just bring it back.

This was what she hated: being treated like an invalid. Being told where to sit and what to do and how much to sleep and what to eat and that she was overdoing it.

Feeling less than.

Being less than.

She silently got into the passenger seat and buckled her seat belt. Marc reached over and touched her arm. "You okay?"

She nodded and rested the side of her head against the window as her mom continued to lecture her about how she needed to stay on the couch or in bed for the next several days. Marc began to drive.

For the umpteenth time that day, Brooke wished she hadn't told Dean to stay home. Wished he were here. There was so much she wanted to tell him. There were so many questions to ask.

Had he really driven her to the clinic? He obviously had, and it cut her up inside thinking what it must have done to him. She had to apologize for causing him all that pain.

Dean was a good man. The kind of man she wished she could have. If things were different...if she could just go back to life before the stroke. Back when she'd taken her good health for granted and never could have imagined the anxiety she faced now.

Today, Dean had gotten a taste of what life with her would look like, and it wasn't pretty.

She wouldn't put him through it. She loved him too much.

Yes, she loved him.

At some point today, in between the ambulance and the tests, she'd realized her feelings had leaped to love.

But nothing had changed—she still couldn't give him forever.

Something Dr. South said earlier echoed in her mind, though, and wouldn't let go. *Our fears don't necessarily reflect reality.*

She was tired of fearing the worst. Tired of living with this constant burden.

Her family had already told her they'd watch the twins tomorrow. She planned on getting out her Bible and her journal and figuring out how to find peace or at least manage the anxiety better.

What she really needed to do was thank Dean in person. Find out how difficult driving her to the clinic had been. Apologize for putting him through it.

But under no circumstances could she tell him she loved him.

She'd keep her feelings tucked deep down inside where they were safe. For Dean's sake. And her own.

Chapter Twelve

Later that night, Dean sat on the couch, staring at the locket in his hand. It had been a day of revelations, and he fully intended to get closure on this, too.

Something told him he'd never be able to truly move forward until he faced his past.

Yet he couldn't bring himself to open the locket. When he did, he'd be unleashing the memories he'd shut away for years.

Finishing the basement had taken a few hours. Every box was emptied, every pile stacked along the wall, taken out to the trash or loaded into the back of his truck to donate. At this point, he was practically on a first-name basis with the staff of the thrift store in Casper, where he'd dropped off so much stuff.

He'd swept and mopped the vinyl flooring down there and arranged the furniture to function as a family room. He couldn't wait for his dad to be released. The man was going to burst with excitement when he saw the basement.

Maybe bursting with excitement wasn't a good thing—he did have a heart problem. Dean chuckled at his own joke. He was willing to take his chances.

He'd texted Marc several times, and Marc had called him before the hospital released Brooke. The tests concluded she hadn't had a stroke, and Dean had almost sunk to his knees in relief.

He'd wanted to call her. But he hadn't. Couldn't bear to hear her clipped words or dismissive tone. He'd already heard both at the clinic. And a text wouldn't work, either. What if he asked her how she was doing and she answered with a thumbs-up emoji or something? He couldn't handle being brushed off as if they hadn't grown close. As if he hadn't told her his darkest secrets. As if they hadn't kissed and opened up about how scared they were to consider a future with anyone else in it. So he hadn't reached out to her at all.

Was that worse? Did she think he didn't care? Did she think about him at all?

At this point, it would be easier to open the stupid locket than to beat himself up about Brooke.

Closing his eyes, he took a moment to clear his mind. Then he looked down at the trinket in his hand. Flipped it over once. Twice. And using both thumbs, he popped it open.

On the right-hand side, his mother smiled back at him. Brown waves of hair fell to her shoulders, and she looked so young and impossibly full of life.

A piercing pain shot through his heart. Why had she left? Why hadn't she come back?

When he was younger, he'd asked himself the same questions—and he'd always answered, *Because of this*.

And by *this*, he meant the left-hand side of the locket.

The three of them together, back when they'd been a family. Dad stood next to his mother. Neither smiled. Dean stood in front, seven years old, grinning like an idiot. It had been taken in town at the Fourth of July festival.

There was a big, black X marked through the picture.

He'd made the X.

After his parents separated, Dean had permanently stopped grinning like an idiot. His safe world had evaporated like a wisp of smoke. He remembered begging his mom to let him live with her. But she'd had other plans.

The night she'd sat him down and told him she was moving far away and that he was staying here with his father, Dean had felt a betrayal so deep, he couldn't see straight. He'd snuck into his parents' room, tiptoed past all the boxes she'd been packing, found the travel bag with her jewelry and taken exactly what he'd been looking for.

The locket.

When he was growing up, his mom had worn it all the time. But she'd stopped wearing it after they split up. Dean had been full of rage when he'd slashed that X with permanent marker.

He'd regretted it immediately. Had slipped it into his pocket and run to his room, crying until he'd fallen asleep.

Not long after, she'd said her goodbyes. He'd wanted so badly to give the locket back to her, to tell her to open it to remember him, but how could he? He'd ruined it.

His anger had ruined everything.

The first year after the divorce, she'd visited him a few times. And he'd always wondered if she'd known he'd stolen the locket. He'd worried she'd tell him he was the one who'd crossed out their family, not her.

With it nestled in his hand, he could see the situation through older, more objective eyes. He wasn't an eight-year-old kid anymore. And his mother hadn't stayed away over a ruined picture in a locket.

She'd wanted out—out of her marriage, out of being a mother—and nothing would have changed it.

Dean closed the locket and shook his head. What a day.

All the things that had been holding him back for so many years… It was as if the walls of Jericho had fallen down.

His mom hadn't cut him out of her life because he'd crossed out their picture.

And he hadn't been trying to kill Lia all those years ago when he'd driven so fast. Yes, he'd driven recklessly, and he'd paid a steep price for it.

But he had to stop punishing himself.

God, You've forgiven me. It doesn't change my stupid choices or the mistakes I've made, but I don't have to keep punishing myself for them anymore. I'm ready to move on. Please, help me.

What if he had another panic attack the next time he tried to drive with a passenger next to him?

So be it. He'd have to trust God with it. Today, his panic symptoms hadn't stopped him in an emergency situation. He'd driven Brooke—white-knuckled—to the clinic. He'd driven the girls—slower than a snail crossing a highway, but he'd done it—back home.

He'd done a lot of things he hadn't thought possible since arriving in Jewel River. Gotten involved with McCaffrey Construction when his father needed him. Kept his word and cleaned out the basement. Finished Brooke's remodeling projects.

Maybe he wasn't such a bad guy after all.

He flipped the locket into the air and caught it. He felt lighter, more hopeful, freer than he could remember. And he recalled those words his dad had told him all those years ago about his temper. Dad had been right. At twenty-one, Dean had thought he knew everything and had chosen the easy path. He *had* let his temper get the best of him.

But the past decade had changed him. The years had taught him patience and humility. He not only could but *would* keep a lid on his anger if it neared the boiling point.

He'd been through too much, punished himself too much, to ever let it get that far again.

Dean stood and took in the glow of the lamp in the darkened room as he made his way to the bedroom. He stopped in front of the dresser, preparing to put the locket back in there. Instead, he clasped it tightly.

Why keep it? He didn't need to cling to guilt or shame. Reaching into his pocket, he pulled out his pocket knife and poked the blade along the edge of the photo with the X until it popped out. He repeated it on the other side. Then he stared at both pictures for a moment and returned to the kitchen. Threw them into the trash.

Without overthinking it, he slid his feet into sliders and made his way outside in the cold air to the back of his truck. He tossed the empty locket into one of the donation boxes.

Someone else could fill it with photos that meant something to them. It no longer meant anything to him.

Back inside, he grabbed a bottle of water from the fridge and returned to the living room.

Tomorrow was Christmas Eve, and this comfortable, inviting home held no sign of it. Brooke was right about that, too. He might as well put up the Christmas tree and enjoy the season for once.

As he lugged out the decorations that Erica had left on the porch when he'd first arrived, he planned out the next day. First he'd ride Dusty and give the horse some treats. An apple and a carrot ought to do it. Then he'd drive to Casper to visit Dad. Maybe they'd get good news and find out he could come home next week. After Casper, he'd return to Jewel River and pay Brooke a visit.

She might not care about him the way he did her, but he needed to see for himself that she was okay. If he ended up wrapping her in his arms and telling her he loved her, all the better.

He loved the woman, and it might be the last time he had the chance to hold her. Not because he was leaving Jewel River. No, Christy's words from this afternoon had seeped inside him and made him realize he wanted a life right here in the community he'd once belonged to. He wasn't sure how it would all work out, but he didn't need to know at this point.

He missed his dad. Missed Marc. Wanted to hang out with Ty and Trent and the other friends he'd grown up with. Was ready to live in a comfortable home like this one rather than a sterile, tiny cabin.

No more hiding away from life on a ranch in Texas. He'd forgotten how much he enjoyed working in construction. And how nice it was to live in a place where everyone knew him. He liked being able to grab a burger from Dixie B's and run into familiar faces.

More than anything, he finally liked himself again.

After ten long years, it was about time.

Brooke woke with a start, jerking upright in her bed. The clock glowed 5:08 in the darkness. For some reason, Reagan's voice kept echoing in her mind. *Praise God. Praise God.*

Were the twins all right? She padded down the hall and into their room. Megan must have climbed out of her crib and into Alice's. A few stuffed animals were piled up on the floor nearby. Those girls were too smart for their own good. They were sleeping with their arms wrapped around each other—her babies, her sweethearts.

Not wanting to wake them, she quietly made her way back to her bedroom. She doubted she'd be able to get back to sleep. She felt keyed up. And no wonder. Yesterday had been all kinds of awful. By the time her family had dropped her off and made sure she had everything she needed, she'd been too tired to function. She'd hugged and thanked Christy, checked on the sleeping twins, crawled into bed and fallen asleep.

She checked her phone. There were several text messages she'd missed yesterday, but none were from Dean. She frowned. She had a lot of smoothing over to do with him. He must be upset. And she'd be mad too if she were him. To think of all he'd done for her, and she'd been so curt with him at the clinic.

She opened the text from her best friend, Gracie. It made her smile.

Reagan called and told me what happened. I'm driving to Jewel River on Christmas Day. I'll stay with your mom if you don't have room for me.

Tears pressed against the backs of her eyes. She had the most supportive group of friends and family on the planet. She texted Gracie back. There's always room for you here. Thank you!

How had she been blessed with so many people who would drop anything to help her out? Her mom, her brother, Reagan, Christy, Gracie—anyone in Jewel River.

And Dean. His selflessness, his generosity, the way he made her feel—like she wasn't a ticking time bomb ready to have a stroke at any minute—had her wanting more.

The enormity of the past three years slammed into her. All she'd been through. All she'd done to move forward. All she'd taken for granted.

God, Reagan was right. Her first instinct was to praise You. And what did I do? Sat there like a sullen child. Mad that I have health issues. Angry that my family was fussing over me. Upset that I can't have the life I want.

Feeling thirsty, she walked through the living room to get to the kitchen. The white Christmas lights still glowed from the tree, and her mother's soft snores drew her attention to the couch. The woman was covered with a thick, soft blanket, and the sight tugged at her heart. Her mom would do anything for her.

Brooke made a mental note to thank her mother and to be more patient.

As quietly as possible, she selected a journal and her favorite Bible from the shelf. Then she poured herself a glass of water and retreated to her bedroom, where she turned on a reading lamp and settled into bed.

It had been a few months since she'd logged any entries in the journal. Staring at the blank page made her pause. What should she write? A diary entry? A list of things to be thankful for? She took a drink as she tried to decide.

At this rate, it would be New Year's Eve before she wrote anything.

She had to start somewhere. And she knew exactly where to begin. The day when everything changed. The day Ross died.

She remembered details from the day like it was yesterday. How sunny and warm it had been. How she'd driven to the supermarket and debated over three flavors of ice cream before purchasing two of them. She'd been hoping Ross would be able to call her. Instead, she'd gotten the news she'd never wanted to hear.

Brooke poured it all out on the pages—the feelings of it not being real, the grief, the depression, the difficulty of those first months as a mom. She had to flex her hand again and again as it cramped while she wrote.

The sun was rising as she wrapped up the journal entry. While she flipped through the pages she'd scribbled, a new-found understanding of herself, her circumstances and God's provision for her took hold.

Lord God, You've held my hand through every step of my life. I don't know what I'd do without my family—Mom, Marc and Reagan. I love them so much.

She'd do anything for them. The same as they'd do for her.

Ross and I didn't have much time together, but I loved him, too. That will never change. Then the twins came along. They gave me so much to do, I didn't have time to think about how much I missed Ross anymore.

She hadn't really allowed herself to think back to those months leading up to the stroke. She'd been too busy moving forward, raising babies. But now she allowed the memories from that terrible time to return. And more pieces locked into place.

Not sleeping. Barely eating. Just getting through each day.

How many times had her mom and Marc begged her to eat more during her pregnancy and in those first months of having the twins home? They'd told her she needed to keep up her strength for the babies. But she'd ignored them. They hadn't understood that everything tasted like cardboard and had the texture of chalk in her mouth. Her clothes had drooped on her bony frame.

Reality slapped her.

She kept acting like the stroke had come out of the blue. Like nothing had caused it. She'd convinced herself that she'd been perfectly healthy and—bam!—the stroke. But that wasn't what had happened. And it was time to face it.

She'd been at least twenty pounds underweight. Her blood pressure had been higher than a mountaintop. She'd been sleep-deprived for almost a year.

Was it really any wonder her body had shut down? When she'd been running on empty for so long?

Dr. South was right. She didn't have the common risk factors that would cause another stroke. However, back when she'd had one, her risk factors *had* been high.

She tapped her pen against her chin.

She'd told Dean she'd never get married again because of her health and her decision to not have more children. But these journal pages told a different story—one Dean had hinted at previously.

Face it, Brooke. You're scared. Your dad left years ago. Then you fell in love with Ross. But he died, and you were alone again. And now you have a good man who might be willing to take a chance on you, but you won't consider a future with him. Why?

Choked up, she dropped her chin to gain her composure.

I don't think I can take another loss.

Had she been using her fear of having another stroke to protect herself from loving—and losing—again?

She owed Dean an apology. And a thank-you. And so much more.

God, I'm tired of taking from my loved ones when all they do is give. And I don't give You credit for all my blessings, either. You gave me healthy twins. I don't have to worry about money. I have friends nearby who constantly look in on me, babysit for me and overall encourage me. Forgive me for taking You and them for granted. Help me show them all how much they mean to me.

Murmurs came from the twins' room. She closed her eyes and smiled. *Praise You, God!*

She stood, stretched her arms over her head and made her way to the girls' room. Only when she reached the doorway did she realize it was Christmas Eve.

The most wonderful time of the year. She smiled to herself.

Something told her better days were coming. Starting today.

Chapter Thirteen

"Merry Christmas Eve, Dad." Dean entered his room at the rehab center. At dawn, he'd ridden Dusty and given the horse a few treats. Then he'd cleaned up and made good time driving to Casper. It wasn't even ten o'clock. "How are you feeling today?"

His father looked as healthy as he had before the heart attack. Maybe healthier. His color was good, he'd slimmed down by at least thirty pounds, and he was wearing a T-shirt and sweatpants that were clearly too big for him.

"I'm great." Dad gave him a hearty hug. "Merry Christmas Eve to you, too."

"You're in an unusually good mood." He was used to his father ranting about how the staff was trying to kill him with the nonstop exercising and small food portions. That and the never-ending complaints about when they would finally let him return to Jewel River so he could do his job.

"They're releasing me today, son. I got the all-clear to return home."

"What?" Dean couldn't imagine a better gift. Unless… this wasn't wishful thinking on his father's part, was it? "Really? Today?"

"Yes." He pointed to the corner, where two transparent plastic bags were filled with clothing. "I've already got my stuff packed. See?"

Dean couldn't believe it. His dad *was* coming home today.

With a quick knock on the open door, his father's social worker, a short woman in her late forties, entered. "Did Ed tell you the good news?"

"He did," Dean said. "Can we get out of here now?"

"Just a few more forms for Ed to sign, and then you can go." She handed his father an iPad and stylus as she instructed him on what to sign and what to initial. Several minutes later, she shook his father's hand and smiled at Dean. "Take the folder with the instructions. He's all yours."

"Merry Christmas," Dean said to her.

She smiled, nodding. "Merry Christmas."

Dad had already hefted the bags.

"Hold up, Dad. Let me get those. You shouldn't be lifting anything."

"That's what you think. I've been lifting weights—supervised strength training, they call it—for a week. I'm supposed to be active. Move it or lose it. That's what they tell me."

It made sense. Dean wasn't going to argue. He motioned for his father to hand him a bag.

His dad beamed all the way down the hall, saying goodbye to nearly every person they came across. Finally, they made it outside and crossed the parking lot to Dean's truck.

"Feels like Christmas, doesn't it?" Dad chucked the bags into the back seat and climbed into the passenger seat. Then he rubbed his hands together. "A little snow, a little sunshine. It's good to be alive."

"I couldn't agree more." Dean gave his dad a grin. "I can't believe they let you go. And today, of all days."

"You're telling me." His eyes crinkled in the corners.

Dean started the truck, and his chest tightened. He hadn't considered that he might be driving his father home. Would he have a debilitating panic attack? Or would he be able to drive through any symptoms?

After a few shaky breaths, he backed out of the spot and began the long drive home.

"I worked so hard this past week," Dad said, "that they agreed I could take care of myself at home. Between you and me, I get tired pretty easy, but that's to be expected. I promised I'd buy a treadmill. I'll order one this afternoon. Now, tell me everything I've missed since we last talked."

On the main road, Dean swallowed the fear clogging his throat and kept the speed at thirty miles per hour. Beads of sweat formed on his forehead.

At least his dad hadn't said a word about how slow he was driving. His heart thumped, but he kept his gaze ahead. "I finished Brooke's house."

"No kidding? The ramp, too?"

He nodded. "She had quite a scare yesterday. I was there. Thought she was having another stroke." He filled his dad in on the details and realized his breathing was almost normal. He lightly pressed the gas pedal.

"Good thing you were there. Anne, Marc and Reagan were here in Casper yesterday. They stopped by to visit me in the morning. Anne snuck me cinnamon rolls, and Reagan left four huge chocolate-covered strawberries."

"They're good people." Dean started to relax. Nothing but rolling hills and prairie for miles. Now was as good a time as any to keep his other promise—to tell Dad about the accident years ago. "I almost couldn't drive Brooke to the clinic."

"Why not?"

"For ten years now, I haven't been able to drive with anyone else in the vehicle. It's the reason I got that job as a ranch hand in Texas."

"What caused it?"

"My stupidity. About six months after I moved to Dallas, I caught Lia kissing Colin—you remember him?" Dean glanced at his father, who nodded. "We were at a bar. It was late. I was the designated driver, and I couldn't wait to leave. I excused myself for a minute and found them kissing. Went from bored to furious in three seconds flat. Told her to get her own ride home. We were both pretty upset. She got in my vehicle. I told her to get out. She refused, so I drove. We argued, and what can I say? You were right. My temper did hurt someone. I kept going faster and faster. Every word she said made me accelerate more until I crashed."

"What happened? Did she…?" Dad's eyebrows formed a V.

"No. She wasn't hurt. But my SUV… I've never seen anything so mangled. I don't know how she walked away without being seriously injured…or worse. I've lived with that image in my head for a decade."

He placed his hand on Dean's arm. "I'm sorry, son."

"I am, too. Her dad fired me. I got a reckless driving ticket. What a joke. I could have killed her, and all I got was a slap on the wrist? Whatever. I lost my job, my friend, my girl and my self-respect all in one night."

"That's why you got the job on the ranch."

He nodded.

"I wish you'd told me. You've been alone all these years, and you didn't need to be. We all make mistakes."

"I haven't been alone. You never gave up on me." Even when they hadn't seen eye to eye, Dad always wanted the best for him.

"Never will, either."

"God's seen me through all of it."

"You can trust Him."

"I don't want to hide my mistakes and my problems anymore. Like I said, after the accident, I couldn't drive with anyone in the vehicle with me. I tried a few times, and it was always the same. I'd gasp for breath, and in my mind, I'd see the wreckage. My heart would pound in my chest. I'd get dizzy. I was always convinced I was going to die. Had full-blown panic attacks."

"That's a lot to deal with."

"Yeah, I kept it all inside. Until recently. I told Brooke. She's— Well, she's special, and I've gotten close to her."

"Wait. Yesterday—you said you drove her to the clinic?"

"I did."

"You didn't have a panic attack?" Hope lined the words.

"No, I definitely had a panic attack."

"How'd you do it, then?"

"I thought her life depended on it. And the twins were in the back seat. I drove through all the symptoms—could barely breathe. Sweat was dripping. My heart was clenching. I kept it slow. And I got them there in one piece."

"That had to be hard. I'm proud of you. I've always been proud of you, but that's really something."

"Thanks."

"And you're driving me now. You seem fine. Are you?"

"I wasn't at first, but now? Yeah, I feel okay."

Neither spoke for several minutes.

"I like Brooke." Dad stared out the window. "I understand why she made her house accessible for a wheelchair. She needs independence, and the stroke took it from her. She needs the assurance she can raise those babies and live on her own."

Dean wished he'd been more understanding about why the remodel was important to her. He *did* understand. But he'd been dismissive, too—and he shouldn't have been.

"I'm thinking about staying in Jewel River, Dad."

His eyes grew round. "Really? You're not putting me on, are you? I can't take that kind of joke. My heart, you know."

Dean chuckled. "Seriously. I've enjoyed overseeing the projects, and in Brooke's case, I also liked doing the actual work. Laying the tile. Building the ramp. Reminded me of working with you all through high school."

"We were a good team. That's why it was hard when you went to work for your girlfriend's dad. I'd been waiting for you to finish up college and work with me again. And I'm sorry I yelled that day. You were right. You did get your temper from me."

"I didn't leave because of you, Dad."

"I know." He frowned, shrugging. "You had a girlfriend and a good offer."

"I don't think it was that, either. I mean, it was a big part of it, but not all."

"What was it then? Why did you leave?"

"I'd buried a lot of pain from when Mom left us. I think I blamed myself. And I wasn't willing to look inward and deal with any of that. Moving to Texas allowed me to escape."

"You weren't the reason she left. I was." He jabbed his thumb into his chest. "Your mother wasn't meant for a small town. She was a social butterfly from Chicago, used to strolling out the door and sitting in a coffee shop down the street. Picking up takeout food at midnight. Catching a movie on a Friday afternoon and again on Saturday night, just because she could."

"I never knew that."

"How could you? I wouldn't talk about her." He shook his head. "I did you wrong, Dean. I didn't know how to talk about your mother. Pretending it didn't happen didn't make it go away."

"It's in the past. I've made my peace with it."

"You forgive me?" Dad asked.

"There's nothing to forgive." He glanced at him. "Do you forgive me?"

"There's nothing to forgive." He grinned. "Now, let's talk about your role in McCaffrey Construction. I say we make it an equal partnership…"

Once they worked out the particulars, Dean turned on the Christmas station, and they caught up on everything that had happened over the past couple of days. Before long, they arrived at his dad's house and were opening the front door.

"Before you go to your room, there's something I want to show you." Dean set his dad's bags on the floor.

"What are you talking about?"

"Come on." Dean led the way to the basement, and when his dad reached the bottom of the staircase, his jaw dropped. He walked forward, turning this way and that to take it all in.

"I can't believe it." He blinked, staring in wonder. "It's clean. All the boxes and bags and piles are gone."

"What do you think? Are you okay with it?"

"Okay? I'm more than okay. I'd let it become a dumping ground for years. You cleared it all out." His face brightened like the sun shining through a break in the clouds. "Knowing all that stuff was down here bothered me. I kept telling myself I'd tackle it a little here, a little there. But it was daunting, so I avoided it. The only time I ventured to the basement was to add more junk I wasn't sure what do with."

"I know exactly what you mean. That's how I felt, too. But I also felt really guilty. You've been asking me to help for years, and I've never taken the time."

"It wasn't your problem."

"But it was yours, and you mean so much to me, Dad. I love you, and I should have helped you with it sooner."

They hugged. "I love you, too, Dean. I'm speechless. I can't get over how clean it is down here. You know what this place needs?"

"What?"

"New furniture." He snapped his fingers. "A big-screen TV. I'm picturing it now. A man cave."

Dean laughed. "I'm always up for buying a new television. *Man cave* has a nice ring to it."

They went back upstairs, and his dad pointed to the hall. "I'm going to rest for a while."

"Good. I'm heading to Brooke's."

"Are you two a thing?"

"I want to be."

"I wish you well."

"Hey, Dad."

"Yeah?"

"Merry Christmas Eve. It's good to have you back."

"Merry Christmas Eve to you, too. It's good to be back."

"What are you doing?" Brooke's mom yawned as she entered the kitchen later that morning. Earlier, Brooke had changed the girls and gotten them each a sippy cup with milk. Thankfully, her mom had been able to get some much-needed sleep after yesterday's drama. "You're supposed to be resting."

Brooke adjusted the heat on the electric griddle and flipped a pancake. She gave her mom a smile so big, her mouth cracked at the corners. "Merry Christmas Eve, Mom. Thanks for staying over."

"Of course I stayed." Her mother bustled across the room, reaching for the spatula. But Brooke held it up and away from her. Mom stepped back and gave her the don't-test-me stare, but Brooke simply shook her head. Mom glared. "Brooke, go rest on the couch. I'll take over from here."

"I'm making pancakes. Why don't you pour yourself a cup of coffee and have a seat?" She pointed the spatula to the stools opposite where she stood at the island. Her mother didn't take orders well, and that was probably the reason Brooke didn't give them very often.

"I don't like this. Yesterday was a big wake-up call. You've been overdoing it, and—"

"Mom," she interrupted in as gentle a tone as she could manage, "I'm okay. It was a migraine. That's all."

"But next time—"

"There might not be a next time."

"But what if there is?" Her eyebrows twisted in worry.

"Then I'm prepared. The house is ready for the worst-case scenario." A sense of peace filled her with strength. "I can't spend every minute of my life worrying about having another stroke."

Her mom let out a humph, poured herself a mug of coffee and took a seat on the stool. Megan and Alice ran into the room.

"Gwammy!" They wrapped their arms around her mom's legs.

"Oh, my little darlings." She kissed the tops of their heads.

"Are you getting hungry?" Brooke leaned over to see their reactions. Wide-eyed, they nodded. "Good. We're having yummy pancakes. And we're going to sing Christmas songs and color pictures and watch cartoons."

"Yay!" They clapped and hopped up and down.

"But first, I have to finish making these." She straightened, and her heart burst with love for her babies. "Go have a seat at your table."

They scampered off and took a seat. Her mom got up and gave them each a wooden puzzle to play with while they waited. Then she returned to her spot at the island.

"Mom?"

"What, hon?" She sipped the coffee.

"I'm making some changes."

"Don't ask me to get behind anything that's going to hurt your health." She shook her head, her mouth drawn into a tight line.

"Why are you assuming I would want to hurt my health?"

"I'm not." She sighed. "I just… I worry about you."

"I know." The pancakes were golden. She slid them onto a plate, dolloped butter on the griddle and poured batter for new ones. Maybe she needed to approach this conversation from a different angle. "Why didn't you ever remarry?"

Her mom sputtered into her coffee, set the mug down with a thunk and pounded her fist into her chest as she coughed. "What?"

Talk about being dramatic.

"After Dad left, you never got close to anyone. Why?"

"I was busy. The bakery took up all my time."

"Even after we grew up? Marc was busy running the ranch. I fell in love with Ross. Moved out of state. You had time then."

"Dating wasn't on my radar. After your dad left us, Marc and I went into survival mode. It took years to get to a place of stability. And I really never gave dating much thought. I focused my energy on you kids and the bakery."

Brooke flipped the pancakes. Was that what she wanted her life to become, too? Focusing on the twins to the exclusion of everything else?

"What do you think of Dean?" She wasn't sure why she was asking her mother about him.

"I give him credit for stepping in to help when his dad needed him. Do I wish he was settled, with a career? Yes.

But he's your brother's best friend, and it's none of my business what he does with his life."

"He's not a shiftless drifter."

"I didn't say he was." Her eyebrows rose as she lifted the mug to her lips again. "He's not exactly established, either. We don't know what he'll do once Ed comes home. He might not even know yet."

All good points. If Brooke had her way, Dean would stay right here in Jewel River.

"I hope he stays," Brooke said.

"I wouldn't count on it."

In the past, she would have gotten disheartened at her mother's skepticism. However, today it only reminded her she didn't have all the answers. She could trust God with her future, whether it included Dean or not, whether she had another stroke or not. God would be holding her hand. He'd get her through everything.

"I'm in love with him, Mom, and I think I'm going to tell him."

"In love with him?" She set the mug down. "So soon? What are you talking about? Does he know? Does he feel the same? Is he going to stay here? How does he feel about the twins? He's not ready to be a father. He might not want to be one at all. I don't think you've thought this through. This is all too sudden."

The rapid-fire questions and statements took a minute for Brooke to process, and when she did, they hurt.

"Why do you assume the worst? About him and about me?"

"I'm not. I'm just being realistic."

The clacks of wooden puzzle pieces and the sizzles from the griddle filled her ears. She wasn't sure she even wanted to respond to her mom if this was how the conversation was going to continue.

"I don't want to see you hurt," Mom said softly.

"I know. And don't think I haven't noticed your sacrifices. The past two years especially have upended your life, and I appreciate all you've done to take care of me and the girls. I don't know how I would have managed without you."

"Those weren't sacrifices. I love you. I'm your mother. I'm always here for you."

"I know. But they *were* sacrifices. I think it's time I accept the fact I'm healthy. As healthy as I'll probably ever be. I don't need to be in survival mode anymore. I don't need to spend every day fearing another stroke. I'm taking care of myself, and I think it's time to move forward."

"Wishful thinking won't prevent another stroke from happening."

"No, but let's face it. My body was shutting down when I had the stroke. I'm healthy now."

She transferred the new pancakes to the plate. Then she turned off the griddle and found the syrup. Cut up pancakes and put them on snowmen plates for the girls. After she got them settled in their high chairs, they dipped the bites into syrup and began eating.

Brooke stacked three pancakes on a plate and slid it to her mother, then added three to her own plate and drizzled syrup over them. She rounded the island and sat on the stool next to her mom.

"I don't know if Dean and I have a future," she said, "but he's patient and understanding. He took charge yesterday when I needed him the most. I've gotten to know him, and I…" She couldn't think of what else to add. Shaking her head, she scooped a bite of pancakes on her fork.

"I think it's moving awfully fast." Mom's eyes glistened with worry.

"I agree." She nodded. "But we've both had life experience. I don't want to spend the rest of my life alone, not when I could be really happy with him."

Her mom shifted her gaze to her plate. "That's a good point."

They ate in silence until the girls banged on their trays. "More?"

"Hungry today, huh?" They nodded. "I'll get you some more."

By the time she'd loaded their plates with more cut-up pancakes, her mom had finished breakfast and was watching her.

"What's your plan? With Dean?"

"I don't know yet. I didn't think it would be fair to put a man through a lifetime of worrying I could have a stroke at any minute, but now?" She shrugged.

"What changed?"

"Nothing. Everything. I guess Dean opened my eyes."

"Are Marc and Reagan still picking up the girls at noon?" Mom stood and took her plate to the sink.

"Yeah."

"Invite him over. Talk it out. You'll know what to do."

"Thanks, Mom."

"I'll always be here for you." Her mother came over and hugged her. "No matter what."

"Thank you. I'll always be here for you, too." With tears in her eyes, she exchanged an understanding smile with her mother. "I don't know what I'd do without you."

"I think you should wear your burgundy sweater to talk to Dean. It's your color."

"Oh, yeah?" If her mother was suggesting outfits, Brooke knew she'd be on board with them dating before long. She just hoped Dean would be on board, too.

Chapter Fourteen

Dean's phone dinged as he cut the engine to his truck in Brooke's driveway. She'd sent him a text. Can we talk sometime today?

He grinned. Yeah, they could talk. Right now.

He snatched up the flowers he'd bought from the grocery store. A Christmas bouquet with red and white roses, greenery and silver glittery spiral things. He would have liked to buy her two dozen roses, but this was all they had. It would have to do.

Sometime between dealing with his mother's locket and opening up to his dad about the accident, Dean had changed. He no longer felt unworthy of having a full life—with a career, a home, a community, a wife and two little girls.

Now all he had to do was convince Brooke that she deserved it, too.

After two quick knocks on her front door, Brooke opened it, and her big blue eyes widened at the sight of him. She backed up for him to enter, then closed the door behind him.

"You're here." There was a glow about her that had been missing yesterday. Her dark hair fell in big curls over her shoulders, and she wore a burgundy sweater and dark pants.

"These are for you." He thrust the bouquet into her hands. "Is this a good time to talk?"

He craned his neck to see if the girls and her mom were around. No signs of anyone.

"These are beautiful, and yes, it's a great time to talk." With a gentle smile, she pivoted toward the kitchen. "Marc and Reagan took the girls to the ranch. Mom went home for a nap."

"You're alone?" He followed her until she stopped in front of the sink. She reached up and took a vase from a cupboard and filled it with water. "You're feeling okay?"

"Yes to both." As she trimmed the stems, she sighed. "Dean, I'm so sorry about yesterday. I feel terrible."

For what part? His panic attack while driving? Not wanting him with her at the hospital?

She adjusted the flowers and set the arrangement on the island. "I put you in an awful situation. I can only imagine how terrible it was for you to have had to make the decision to drive me to the clinic."

"It forced me to get real about my problem."

"Why did you do it?" Her soft voice and shimmery eyes lured him closer.

"Because you needed me, and I wasn't going to let you down."

"At what cost, though?" Worry lines creased her forehead as she stepped toward him. She reached up and brushed her fingers along the hairline at his temple.

Her touch, her words, her demeanor made his heart pound. This was why he loved her. She was more concerned with him having to drive her than she was with her own health.

"I won't deny I had a panic attack. I could barely see straight in the driveway. Then I glimpsed Meggie and Alice in the back. They looked scared. I couldn't let them—or you—down, so I forced myself to drive. It was slow going, but I got you there. God got us there."

"I will never put you through that again."

"I know you won't." He grinned, reaching for her hand. "Because when I drove them home, it was easier. I still drove slowly, but I didn't have a complete breakdown."

"You mean it?" She searched his eyes. "You could drive me somewhere right now and not be affected?"

"I can't say I wouldn't be affected, but yeah, I could drive you." He brought the back of her hand to his lips. "I have so much to tell you, but first, what did the tests show? What did the doctors say?" He led her to the living room, where they sat side by side on the couch with her hands in his.

"The tests confirmed Dr. South's suspicions. It was a migraine with aura. A bad one. I now have migraine medicine on hand in case it happens again."

"So there won't be any long-term issues? Do you have to do anything different?"

"No and no. Rest for the next couple days. That's it."

He pulled her into a hug, sinking his fingers into her hair, and whispered against her ear, "Praise God."

She twisted out of his arms. "What did you say?"

"I said, 'Praise God.'"

She covered her mouth with her hands. Then her shoulders shook, and she cried.

What had he said? He wrapped her in his arms, caressing her back and murmuring shushing noises.

He wasn't sure why she was upset, but he'd caused it— he knew that much.

When she regrouped, she wiped the tears away and sniffed. "You probably think I'm a mess."

"No."

"Reagan said the same thing last night when we learned it wasn't a stroke. She kept saying, 'Praise God.'"

It didn't seem out there to him that they would all want to praise God for her health, but what did he know?

"I realized how tight-fisted I am with my praise to God. My first thought was that this time it was a migraine, but what about next time? I was angry for having to live in constant fear. But Reagan—and Marc and Mom and all of my friends, and now you—are thankful it wasn't worse news."

"We're thankful you're alive, Brooke. You're a special person. Of course we're going to praise God that He watched over you and kept you safe from harm."

"I know, and I feel so ashamed. Because I should be the one praising Him. I woke up early this morning—before dawn—and I took out a journal and really thought over the past couple of years. They've been so hard. And blaming everything on the stroke was easier than accepting the other fears I have."

"Like what?"

"You already know. You called me out on it last week. I'm afraid of being left behind. Of loving someone and losing them. My dad saw no reason to be a part of my life. And Ross died when we'd barely gotten started."

"I'm sorry, Brooke. You've been through so much."

"You have, too."

"Not like you have." He wanted to kiss her, but he had things to say. "I understand why you needed to remodel the house. The ramp is done, by the way."

"It is? Completely?" She brightened. "I forgot to even check."

"Yes. And I also understand why you've decided marriage is off-limits."

"Yeah, about that—"

"But yesterday and today have given me a whole new perspective. And I'm not leaving until I convince you that you can trust me with your forever. I love you, Brooke. And nothing's going to change it."

* * *

Her sharp intake of breath kicked up her adrenaline. Dean loved her?

"But you saw what happened to me." She lowered her chin, needing to be transparent with him. "Everything I experienced yesterday was similar to a stroke."

"I know, and I want to be the one here in case it happens again. I don't want you to be alone. I don't want to be alone. I've been alone for ten long years, Brooke, and I'm tired of living like that. You changed me."

"Why?" She didn't know what she was asking. All she knew was up until yesterday, he'd refused to consider forever. And she'd refused, too.

His lips curved slightly, and his eyes crinkled in the corners. "Turns out coming back to Jewel River was exactly what I needed. I've had to make peace with things I'd been running from."

"The accident?" She moved closer to him, wanting his arms around her again, but content to watch him as he talked.

"Yes, but other things, too. The basement was part of it. I found something of my mother's down there that I'd been avoiding. It forced me to admit I'd believed I was the reason she left. But I was just an eight-year-old kid. I've let that go."

She nodded in understanding.

"But Dad—did I even tell you he's home?"

"No, really? What terrific news!"

"Yeah, they released him this morning. He was blown away when I showed him the basement. He's online shopping right now for a treadmill and a big-screen TV. Said it's going to be the man cave."

She chuckled, even though she wanted to get back to the subject at hand. The two of them. Love.

"Anyway," Dean continued, "I told him about what happened in Texas. And I told him I'm staying here in Jewel River. I'm ready to have a life again."

Hope almost choked her. He was staying!

"Listen, Brooke." He caressed the back of her hand with his thumb. "I get your fear about having another stroke, and I'm sorry I was dismissive the other day. I didn't fully understand what you're up against and how difficult it is to live with that kind of fear."

He was saying everything she'd needed to hear, and she loved him all the more for it.

"I'm not living like that anymore," she said.

"What do you mean?"

"You faced your fears and your past, and I did the same. I've been lying to myself. I wasn't healthy when I had the stroke. You can ask Marc or my mom. I'd lost a ton of weight, wasn't eating, wasn't sleeping. My body couldn't take it anymore. And all this time, I've convinced myself I could have another stroke any day—and truthfully, I could—but the doctors have assured me I've kept my risk factors to a minimum. I need to trust God with this, Dean. I need to let go of this constant worry."

"What are you going to do?"

"I'm going to praise God." She closed her eyes briefly as the sweet rush of peace stole over her. "Every morning, I'm going to praise Him for another day. And I'm going to trust Him. If I have another stroke, I know He'll take care of me. I'm done limiting my life."

She searched his eyes and saw nothing but admiration. Squeezing both his hands in hers, she held his gaze. "I love you, Dean. Your courage and generosity humble me. I know how tough it was for you to come back. All the worrying about your father. Then you took on his construction projects. None of that was easy. And I'll always be in your debt for driving me and the girls to the clinic. You're the best guy I've ever met, and I don't deserve you, but I love you. I promise you if you'll give me a chance, I'll do everything I can to make you happy."

He crushed her to him, and she sank into his embrace, grateful beyond measure he'd come into her life.

Then his hands lightly framed her cheeks, and he was kissing her. She kissed him back, pouring all her emotions into it. Sensing his conviction. This was a man who would never let her down, never walk way, never give up on her.

When they ended the kiss, she took a minute to regroup. "I never asked how you felt about the twins."

"You don't have to." He shook his head. "I love them. They wriggled into my heart from day one."

Just as she'd hoped. But there was one more issue to address, and it was important. "The doctors advised me not to have more children. It would be too dangerous."

"You already have two beautiful girls." His face broke into a smile. "I'd say that's a good-sized family."

"I would have liked more," she admitted, enjoying the way he was stroking her back.

"I never thought I'd get married, let alone have kids, so as far as I'm concerned, the twins are the icing on the cake."

"Are we talking about marriage?" she asked, surprised she'd already accepted the thought.

"If not now, we will be soon, I hope."

She didn't have a chance to respond. He'd claimed her lips with his again. And nothing else mattered.

Chapter Fifteen

"Hey, Marc, can we talk for a minute?" Dean pulled Marc from the crowd after the Christmas Eve service that night. Brooke held Megan on her hip, and Anne held Alice. The girls were wearing frilly dresses, white tights, shiny black shoes and ribbons in their hair. To say they were cute would be an understatement. A group of people stood in a circle talking to Dean's dad, and every now and then, Ed's hearty laugh filled the air.

"Sure, what's up?"

They retreated to the coat rack, where a few stragglers were zipping up before heading to the door.

"I hate to have this conversation here, but I wanted a word before we head over to Brooke's," Dean said.

"What's going on?" His expression shifted from merry, like the holiday signaled, to worried in a split second.

"I'm in love with your sister." He probably shouldn't have blurted it out like that, but he'd been holding it in for hours. This was a conversation he needed to have in person with his best friend, the man who'd been there for him since he was a child.

Marc blinked a few times, and Dean held his breath, unsure if he would be upset or okay with the situation. Then a grin slowly stretched across his face, and Dean relaxed.

"That's great!" Marc pulled him in for a bear hug. Then he stepped back, nodding with twinkling eyes. "Does she know?"

"Yeah, we had a long talk this afternoon."

"And she's on board with…what exactly is happening between you two?"

"She's on board. We're dating. More than that, really. I love her, and she loves me, and I plan on proposing in the near future."

He let out a low whistle. "You aren't messing around, are you? Do you think you might be rushing it? Brooke has been pretty clear that she doesn't want to get remarried. I'd hate for you to get your hopes up."

"The past few days have changed her mind. And if she needs to go slow, I'll wait as long as it takes. I love her, and I'm not letting her go."

"Good. She's worth the wait." He adjusted his necktie, looking like he wanted to yank it off and toss it in the trash. "Does this mean you're staying in Jewel River?"

"Yeah. Dad and I worked out a plan. I'm officially becoming a partner after the new year."

"Yes!" Marc pumped his fist in the air. "Where are you going to live?"

"I'd like to keep renting Reagan's house if she's okay with it."

"She'll be thrilled. She doesn't like seeing it empty." He shook his head in wonder. "I feel like I just won a million bucks. You're moving back. Dating my sister. Merry Christmas to me."

Dean chuckled. "I'm the one who's the winner. Thank you, man. Thanks for all the ways you were there for me through the years."

The Christmas Eve service had touched him—the fact

God would send His Son to save a sinner like him made his heart burst with gratitude. His empty, closed-off life had become full. Full of light, energy, opportunities and love. He didn't deserve it, but he sure was grateful for it.

"Are you ready?" Brooke came over. "The twins are getting restless."

"Let's go." Dean took Megan from her, and she snuggled her cheek onto his shoulder.

Fifteen minutes later, Dean and his father, Anne, Marc, Reagan and the twins sat in Brooke's living room. Anne carried a tray with cookies and bars around to everyone, and Dean helped himself to several.

"I made these special for you, Ed." Anne pointed to some square treats in the corner of the tray. "Pumpkin bars. They're low in sugar."

"Thank you. Those muffins you sent with Dean were some of the best I've ever had. I didn't know healthy could taste so good."

They laughed. Then the twins started yawning. Brook stood. "I'd better get these two in their pajamas. I'll be right back. Come on, girls, let's get your comfy pj's on."

They raced ahead of her to the hallway.

"I'll help." Dean placed his hand against the small of her back as they continued to the girls' bedroom.

She looked at him and smiled. "I can do it by myself, you know."

"I know." He slid his hand around her waist. "But then I'd miss you."

"Miss me?" She laughed. "With everyone back in the living room?"

"I only want to be with you."

She paused in the girls' doorway and turned to him. "I feel the same way."

He tugged her closer and gave her a kiss. Little giggles made them separate. Brooke glanced at Megan and Alice, who were on the floor yanking off their tights.

"Welcome to my world." She shook her head with a smile.

"Your world is the only place I want to be."

"Then come on in." She waved him into the room.

"You don't have to ask me twice."

"Praise God."

Praise Him, indeed.

Epilogue

"He's going to make a good daddy."

Brooke followed Christy Moulten's gaze to where Dean stood talking to Marc, Cade and Dalton in the community center. The blustery February evening hadn't deterred the Jewel River Legacy Club members from gathering. Her mom was watching the twins so Brooke and Dean could make their announcement.

"He certainly is." Brooke gave Christy a smile.

"I wish Ty would find someone. Every month I remind him of the meeting time. And every month he avoids it. Not that he's going to find a girlfriend at the Legacy Club, but he should be getting out more." Christy made a clucking sound with her tongue. "At least Cade found his forever love. With Cade and Mackenzie married, maybe they'll think about having babies."

"I hope so." Brooke had enjoyed their wedding last month, probably because Dean had been her date.

Erica Cambridge stood at the podium and waited until she had everyone's attention. Dean slid into the seat next to Brooke's, and he slung his arm around her shoulders. He was always nearby, which was just one of the many things she loved about him. She could count on him.

His father sat on his other side. Ed was thriving now that

he was back home. He'd bought a treadmill, converted the basement into a man cave and thrown himself back into Mc-Caffrey Construction with gusto.

"Sorry to bring you out on a cold night like this, but it's Wyoming, right?" Erica opened her hands as if to say, *What can you do?* "Clem, would you mind getting the meeting started?"

He stood and led them in the Pledge of Allegiance and the Lord's Prayer. After everyone had settled in their seats, Erica went over meeting minutes and old business.

"Erica?" Angela Zane raised her hand.

"Yes, Angela?"

"What are we going to do about the meat market closing?"

"I talked to Bob at the supermarket, and he assured me they'll continue to stock local beef and pork."

"What about the building, though? I had this idea—"

Clem raised his palm. "Don't say it."

Angela shot him a glare. "As I was saying, I had an idea. For a meat locker."

"A meat locker?" Erica looked confused.

"Yes. It's like a storage unit for your meat. For anyone who doesn't have enough freezer space."

"Everyone has enough freezer space." Clem narrowed his eyes.

"Actually, that isn't true." Ed joined the conversation. "You'd be surprised at how many people don't have enough room to store their frozen meat. A quarter cow takes up a lot of space."

Angela's chin rose, and she sent Clem a smug look. "Joey and I discussed it at length during last month's storm, and he took the liberty of making a promo video."

"Not another video." Clem shook his head. "Does your grandson ever study?"

"He's on the honor roll." She took out her phone. "Let me send you the video, Erica."

While Erica and Dalton got the screen and equipment ready, Dean leaned over to Brooke. "What's going on?"

"I'm not sure. But if Joey's involved, it means there will be some explosive special effects."

Christy turned her head and gave them a thumbs-up. "I was hoping Joey would have something for us tonight. Livens things up."

The lights went out, and the screen glowed with an outside view of the meat market. A man's low voice narrated. "No meat market? No problem. Jewel River has a whole new way to store your meat." Lightning bolts crisscrossed the screen while the sound of thunder boomed. "Ice lockers. Big. Small. For a bag of wings or a full deer. You decide."

Dynamite blasts erupted, and an animated Coming Soon banner unfurled across the screen.

Erica turned on the lights. "Marc, you're on the town planning committee. What do you think?"

Marc launched in on the permits involved. Brooke yawned. It had been a long day, and she really wanted to make their announcement and head back to her place to snuggle up on the couch with Dean and watch a TV show.

When the meeting was about to wrap up, Erica asked if there were any announcements. Dean rose and helped Brooke stand.

"We have an announcement." Dean looked around the room. "Brooke and I are engaged. I asked her to marry me over the weekend, and she accepted."

Congratulations filled the air. When the chatter died down, Ed stood, too.

"I'm thankful to finally have a daughter." Ed's eyes were moist as he beamed at Brooke. "And granddaughters. I'm a blessed man. Also, the paperwork has been finalized. Dean and I are officially partners at McCaffrey Construction."

Everyone stood to congratulate them, and when the meeting ended, Brooke took Dean's hand as they made their way out the door.

Her leg had been weak all day, but she wasn't letting it worry her. She'd taken it easy and was more than happy to lean on Dean's strong arm at times like this.

"Are you okay?" He looked into her eyes, tightening his grip on her hand.

"Yes. Thank you."

Out in the cold wind, he put his hands around her waist and swept her off her feet in a twirl. "I love you, Brooke."

She laughed, her hands resting on his shoulders, and kissed him. "I love you, too."

"I can't wait for you to be mine."

"News flash, Dean. I'm already yours."

His grin said it all. He kissed her again.

"And I'm yours. Praise God, I'm all yours."

* * * * *

If you enjoyed this Wyoming Legacies story, be sure to pick up the previous books in Jill Kemerer's miniseries:

The Cowboy's Christmas Compromise
United by the Twins
Training the K-9 Companion

Available now from Love Inspired!

Dear Reader,

I hope you enjoyed this Christmas story. Brooke and Dean struggled through valid fears that affected their everyday lives. Brooke believed she would have another stroke at any moment, while Dean believed he would cause another accident if he drove with a passenger. Brooke didn't keep her fear a secret, but Dean kept his locked deep inside, not wanting anyone to know how badly he'd messed up all those years ago.

By spending time together, trusting each other and praying through the moments when their worst fears seemed to be coming true, they were able to trust God and accept that He'd help them live with their fears.

Like Brooke, we can praise God even when our situation doesn't change, and we're facing an uncertain future. I pray you'll give the good Lord your worries this Christmas season and enjoy the peace only He can offer.

I hope you enjoyed this book in the Wyoming Legacies series. I love connecting with readers. Feel free to email me at jill@jillkemerer.com or write me at P.O. Box 2802, Whitehouse, Ohio, 43571.

Blessings to you!
Jill Kemerer

HARLEQUIN
Reader Service

Enjoyed your book?

Try the perfect subscription for Romance readers and get more great books like this delivered right to your door.

See why over 10+ million readers have tried Harlequin Reader Service.

Start with a Free Welcome Collection with free books and a gift—valued over $20.

Choose any series in print or ebook.
See website for details and order today:

   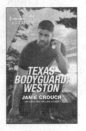

TryReaderService.com/subscriptions

RSBPA24R